"I see you don't [ ] enough to keep [ ] buggy."

Malachi buckled the halter, and then the oat bag, over Kip's head. "I've been doing a number of things over the past few days. Thinking about blankets hasn't been very high on the list."

Ruth huffed. "Wisconsin weather will take a heavy toll on the unprepared."

"Unprepared? Like not having dog food when you have a dog?"

Ruth scooped up the puppy that trailed at her heels and crossed to Malachi, her hand outstretched for the grocery bags. He shook his head and retained possession of them.

"I'll help you get to the house. With this wind and your small sizes, the two of you could end up in the next county."

Aware that he had a point, she didn't argue. They headed for the exit. "I...I want to thank you for going out of your way and following me home, even though I didn't need it."

"You're welcome." Ruth could hear the smile in his voice.

Growing up on a farm, **Jocelyn McClay** enjoyed livestock and pursued a degree in agriculture. She met her husband while weightlifting in a small town—he "spotted" her. After thirty years in business management, they moved to an acreage in southeastern Missouri to be closer to family when their eldest of three daughters made them grandparents. When not writing, she keeps busy hiking, bike riding, gardening, knitting and substitute teaching.

Books by Jocelyn McClay

Love Inspired

The Amish Bachelor's Choice

Visit the Author Profile page at Harlequin.com.

The Amish Bachelor's Choice

Jocelyn McClay

Recycling programs
for this product may
not exist in your area.

LOVE INSPIRED BOOKS

ISBN-13: 978-1-335-47931-0

The Amish Bachelor's Choice

www.Harlequin.com

Printed in U.S.A.

For I know the thoughts that I think
toward you, saith the Lord, thoughts of peace,
and not of evil, to give you an expected end.
—*Jeremiah* 29:11

First, I thank God for this amazing opportunity. Thanks always to my wonderfully supportive husband, Kevin. Thanks also to my beta readers, particularly Alyson, who noted to the Iowa crew that my interest in romance novels was more than just a way of avoiding doing dishes years ago. But this is for you, Genna. I couldn't have done it without you. May there be many more to come.

Chapter One

"I wonder if the new owner will change the name? It'd be strange to have it no longer be Fisher Furniture." Jacob's words were barely audible over the humming of the lathe.

The blood drained from Ruth Fisher's face. She hadn't considered that possibility. *Oh,* Daed, *if missing you wasn't enough, how can I bear to see your name removed from the business you built?* The end of her nose prickled as she swallowed against the lump in her throat.

Widening her eyes against threatening tears, Ruth willed her coworker not to look up from his focus on the spinning chair leg until she eliminated any trace of the effect his words had had on her. She glanced around the workshop to ensure the few others working in the extensive room weren't paying attention, before tipping her head back and blinking any telltale traces away. No one would see her cry.

The others understood her grief. Friends and neighbors as well as employees of her father's furniture business had helped her through his difficult passing and funeral. But they were moving on. When Ruth moved on, it would be away from her *daed*'s legacy. She'd made a promise. She swallowed again, this time against a flash of nausea at the reminder of her recent resolution. It took pinching the skin between her thumb and forefinger to stop any renegade tears. But when Jacob looked up, he was met with clear eyes behind her safety glasses.

"*Ach*, Ruth, I—I thought you were Isaac," he stammered, his face flushing to match his red hair.

"He was busy, so I brought the chisels over." She set them on the bench beside him.

"I—I… It was on my mind as they moved in this weekend."

Ruth didn't have to ask who "they" were. Jacob's family farm was a mile from the Yoder farmstead, empty since Atlee died last winter. Empty until the new owner of Fisher Furniture had bought it.

"My *daed* and brothers stopped by to see if they needed any help. *Mamm* and Lydia took a basket of bread and canned goods." Jacob was obviously excited at the prospect of new neighbors. "Lydia was glad to see that none of the three newcomers had beards."

Ruth could just imagine. If none of the men had beards, then they were all single. Jacob's sister was in her *rumspringa*. Potential courtship and future mates were much on a young woman's mind during her run-around years. Particularly a girl like Lydia.

"Hopefully they are good workers, beardless or no." Ruth had different priorities. Even though she'd no longer be part of the business, she wanted to see it succeed.

"How are the chairs coming for the Portage order?" They had recently entered into business with a furniture dealer in one of the larger towns nearby.

Jacob's eyes lit up. "*Gut.* I like this design. Hopefully it sells well."

"*Ja*, hopefully," she echoed, forcing a smile to her face before turning to head for her own workbench.

Once there, Ruth selected a piece of oak from the neat stack on the scarred wooden surface and picked up a sanding block. She'd hoped for a number of things. She'd even had the *hochmut* to pray that someone in the district would purchase the business. The glasses slipped down her nose when she winced at the memory that she'd had the arrogance to tell *Gott* what to do. It wouldn't happen again. Ruth wrinkled her nose in an effort to push the glasses back up. Well, it shouldn't happen again. One of the tenets of their faith was *demut*. There was certainly no humility in daring to give *Gott* instructions. Thankfully, *Gott* was forgiving as well as good. He had a plan for her. But apparently it didn't include having someone she knew buy Fisher Furniture and letting her manage it. This Malachi Schrock had certainly wasted no time in taking over her *daed*'s business.

Her shoulders slumped as she ran the block over the oak. No single young woman in their district owned a business that employed four men, married and single. The bishop wasn't going to allow Ruth to be the first, even though she'd worked beside her father from the time she was tall enough to reach a workbench.

Or not tall enough, Ruth remembered with a tremulous smile. *Daed* had built her a little wooden box to stand on. First, so she could watch him work, her eyes wide with wonder at his deft movements. Then so she could mimic his actions and learn to love the wood, from its first rough surfaces to the feel of it beneath her fingers, soft as a baby's cheek after multiple cycles of sanding and varnish.

The sale of the business had been the topic of several conversations after church service two weeks ago. While gossiping was frowned upon in the Amish community, sharing of news was another thing entirely. At least three groups of folks Ruth had passed as she poured coffee for the noon meal had been discussing Miriam Lapp's nephew from Ohio, who'd purchased the business and would soon be moving into the area, along with two of his younger brothers.

Ruth was chagrined to discover, when she overheard people talking after church yesterday, that her life continued to be a subject of interest. This time, the discussion among the women, and probably some of the single men, was when she'd marry, now that her father was gone and the business sold. A few speculative glances had been cast her way when certain names were mentioned, gauging her reaction.

Ruth had made sure her normally expressive face revealed nothing.

Jacob's name was one mentioned with a side-glance yesterday. Ruth's lips twitched. According to her newly married friends, finding it hard to breathe around a man was a sign he might be *Gott*'s Chosen One for her. She had no difficulty breathing around Jacob, whom she'd known since back when she could wear buttons. He was nothing more than a casual friend, and the only time he made her heart beat harder was when she observed and appreciated his skill on the lathe. The women of the district could speculate all they want, but she wouldn't be walking out with Jacob Troyer.

Her smile faded. She wouldn't be walking out with any Amish man now that she was leaving the community as she'd promised her *daed*.

Ruth grabbed a tack cloth and swiped it across the oak's surface, surprised she hadn't worn a hole in the wood. She stroked a thumb along the grain. Today, not even working with the wood brought her the peace and joy it normally did.

But peace required *gelassenheit*. Submission didn't come naturally to Ruth. Sometimes it didn't come at all. Putting down the cloth, she picked up the sanding block and deftly applied it. Inhaling deeply, she relished the aroma of fresh lumber inherent to the room. *Gelassenheit*. Bits of sawdust danced in the air as she exhaled slowly through pursed lips, trying to clear her mind to *Gott*'s will.

So the new owner had arrived in Miller's Creek with his two brothers. Ruth's hand paused, her eyes resting on the other occupants of the room. Her heart beat heavily as she wondered what the addition of three more men would mean for her father's loyal employees. The strokes across the wood resumed with jerky motions.

Ruth didn't know what she needed to do, but she was determined that the men would keep their jobs. Dropping the block on the counter, Ruth folded her hands in her lap and bowed her head. She would pray and accept *Gott*'s will for her fellow workers and herself.

Ruth squeezed her eyes shut. Hopefully His will would journey the same road as her plans.

The horse flicked his ear back toward the buggy, probably wondering if he was going to get down now that they'd arrived at their destination. Malachi figured the gelding was glad to be hanging its head over the hitching post. He frowned at the foam-flecked brown neck. Experienced with horses, he knew the animals could feel the tension of the driver through the reins. The poor bay had completed a trip full of nervousness running down the lines. No wonder his coat reflected his agitation. Malachi resolved to keep this visit short or find a place where he could stable the standardbred. It was warm for November, but he wouldn't leave a hot horse for long out in it.

Sighing, he set the brake and stepped down from the buggy. As he passed the gelding, he paused to stroke the horse's sleek, sweaty neck. It wasn't the bay's fault. He was fine for a rented animal. Malachi ran a hand down the iron-hard leg to where the brown coat turned to black, smiling when the gelding responded by lifting his hoof.

In fact, he might buy the bay. He and his brothers would need several buggy horses. Samuel would be replacing his courting buggy as soon as they settled in, probably before. Gideon, as well. Malachi shook his head at the thought. His brothers had grown faster than the passing years justified.

His smile faded as he straightened to regard the building in front of him. At least the horse was something he could try out before purchasing. Unlike the small farmstead he'd bought sight unseen. Or the business before him, which he was now owner of. Another deep sigh lifted the suspenders that crossed his shoulders.

He wasn't impulsive. Far from it. Malachi knew himself to be like Barley, one of his father's draft horses back in Ohio. A plodder. Barley hadn't moved fast, but his steady and deliberate pace had plowed, planted and harvested many fields. The seed that'd culminated in Malachi's move to Wisconsin had germinated long ago. Things had been getting difficult back in Ohio. Malachi was surprised he'd survived there this long. Some type of change had been needed. He'd prayed that *Gott* would provide him with direction. When he'd heard of this opportunity, he'd snatched it up like a horse snapping at an insect during blackfly season.

Hopefully this'd been *Gott*'s answer. Once he'd settled on his course, Malachi hadn't paused in his plodding forward long enough to check.

The furniture shop was a good investment. He'd reviewed numbers available on the operation before he'd made the offer. It was a well-run business and Malachi was excited to be part of it. But it was a big change. He wasn't fond of changes. This purchase had prompted several of them in his life. Walking through that door would hopefully wrap up the last and biggest one.

After giving the bay a final rub on the forehead, he headed up the stairs. A cheery jingle greeted him when he swung the door open. Malachi's tense shoulders eased slightly as he inhaled the familiar scents of wood and stain. His lips curved. This was what he knew and loved. It would be all right.

An encompassing glance revealed a well-ordered showroom. His experienced eye recognized the diverse furniture's primary wood as oak, with a few pieces of cherry, maple and walnut. Stepping farther into the airy room, he ran a hand over the back of a chair that tucked into a large dining table. Malachi nodded in approval at the smooth surface. He straightened abruptly and turned to the back of the store when he heard the sound of a door opening.

An Amish woman stepped through, a ready smile on her face. Her auburn hair was tucked under her *kapp*, a few strands threatening to escape the confines. Reaching up, she touched the safety glasses on her face, hastily pulled them off and set them on the sales counter. With flushed cheeks and a sheepish smile, she turned back to him.

"Good morning. May I help you?" she inquired as she approached, her black shoes making no sound on the glossy wooden floor.

He couldn't help returning the smile. Her grin became full and moved to her eyes. Eyes that lifted briefly to his hat before returning to his face. Malachi yanked the black felt from his head and held it in front of him. *"Guder mariye,"* he returned the greeting. "My name is Malachi Schrock. I was told to meet Bishop Weaver here this morning."

The warmth faded from her face like the temperature of a fine October day upon the approach of an early-winter storm. Malachi didn't realize how much he'd appreciated its glow until he was facing frost in her green eyes.

"Ah. The new owner. The bishop isn't here right now. If he told you to meet him, I'm sure he'll be in as soon as he can." Even her voice had changed from June to December.

Malachi raised his eyebrows. The families that'd greeted him and his brothers at the farmstead had been quite cordial. Some of the young women, enthusiastically so. Obviously, this woman worked here. Just as obviously, he wasn't welcome. He slowly shifted the brim of his hat between his hands. Hopefully this attitude wasn't the consensus of his new workforce.

Upon reaching him, the woman clasped her hands together at her waist, regarding him coolly. The top of her head, even with the thick soles on her shoes, barely reached his chin.

"If you have any questions about the business, I'd be… I will answer them for you."

Happy had been the omitted word that hung in the silence of the room. She was *not* happy to have him here, *not* happy to answer his questions. Malachi sighed. He didn't know what he might have done already to offend her. He'd only been in the district a few days and the store a few minutes.

Malachi had never been a business owner before, but he'd run a large furniture operation for his previous employer in Ohio. To his knowledge, all those he'd supervised had been quite content with his leadership. He intended that to be the case here. Apparently, he had some ground to make up.

Glancing back toward the front door, he noted the hat rack at its customary location just inside. Malachi took a moment to put his hat on one of the pegs before turning back to the young woman. He suppressed a smile. She reminded him of a fierce bantam hen.

"What would you like to tell me about the business?"

His mild, open-ended question seemed to surprise her, but she recovered quickly. "It's a well-run operation."

Malachi nodded solemnly. "I noted that from the bookwork."

The ice in her green eyes melted slightly. A shrewd spark began to replace the frost. "The employees are extremely capable and loyal. They've all worked here for some time and are very valuable to the business."

His lips twitched slightly at her artfulness. "That is *gut* to know."

"New accounts have been established with some of the larger *Englisch* furniture stores. We are starting to get a backlog of orders. It's probably time to hire more workers." She eyed him closely, gauging his response.

So this woman knew that his brothers were joining him in the business. Even without telephones, news spread fast in Amish communities. While his brothers would work with him, he had no plans to change the workforce at this time. Not until he understood their abilities and how they benefited the operation. Malachi respected that she was trying to protect the current employees. He also recognized that she was trying to lead him. Plodder he might be, but he didn't like being pulled by the halter. "Are you falling behind?"

Her mouth opened in a perfect circle before snapping closed. "Not at all! I just wanted to assure you that there was ample work to be done."

"*Gut.* I look forward to reviewing the orders." He

regarded her quietly. "You mentioned *we*. How long have you worked here?"

For a moment, her eyes clouded. "My father was Amos Fisher, the previous owner. I can't remember a time when I didn't come to work with him."

Malachi frowned in sympathy for her loss at the same time a chill ran up his spine. A managing female in the business. Just what he'd left Ohio to avoid. He continued his study of the woman in front of him. She returned his scrutiny. Malachi drummed his fingers slowly against his pant leg. Perhaps there would be one immediate change to the workforce after all.

They turned in relieved unison when the door jingled to announce a new arrival.

The tall man who entered nodded to the woman before hanging his hat and extending his hand to Malachi.

"I am Ezekiel Weaver. You are Malachi Schrock?" He continued at Malachi's nod, "Welcome to Miller's Creek. I see you've met Ruth Fisher. I'm sure she was sharing how glad we are that you're coming to live in the community."

"Something like that." Malachi's eyes returned to the young woman's. Her smooth cheeks flushed under his regard.

The bishop dipped his head in approval. "*Gut*. She can tell you a lot about the business."

"So I'm discovering." So the bishop wasn't aware of the young woman's animosity. Malachi wasn't going to be the one to share the news. Except for the situation in Ohio, where evasion had seemed the more prudent choice, Malachi addressed his own battles.

Bishop Weaver turned to the young woman. "Ruth, do you have a place where we can talk in private?"

"Certainly." She gestured to the door of a small office. The bishop entered and shut the door after Malachi joined him, leaving the young woman on the other side. Malachi winced at the expression on her face. Her exclusion from a discussion regarding the business certainly hadn't smoothed any waters for him. The bishop might be glad that Malachi was now in the community, but on the other side of the door was someone who clearly wasn't.

Chapter Two

Ruth's cheeks were so hot they had to be flaming red. Granted, she deserved the ample dose of embarrassment from her behavior toward the new owner. If her *grossmammi* had been alive, she'd have admonished Ruth. *Keep your words soft and sweet. You might have to eat them.* Ruth could almost hear *Grossmammi*'s tranquil voice repeating the Amish proverb.

It hadn't been the words so much, Ruth recalled. The words were true. Her coworkers' jobs were on her mind. When things were on her mind, Ruth expressed them. It'd been the attitude used in delivering the words that would be hard to choke down if served back to her. And the new owner was well within his rights to serve up a banquet.

Ruth banged her head gently against the side of a nearby hutch. Her prayer *kapp* slipped farther down her hair at the contact. She couldn't have made a worse first impression if she'd tried. Reaching behind her head to address the familiar task of repinning the *kapp*, she glanced up and froze. Yes, apparently she could. For meeting her eyes through the window between the office and the showroom were the keen blue ones of the new owner. Ruth jabbed a final pin in her hair, whirled around and swept through the door into the workroom.

It wasn't the heavy bang of the door as she came through that focused all the attention in the workroom on her. They'd obviously been watching for someone to enter. Four sets of curious eyes observed Ruth as she slid her hands down the front of her apron. The noise in the room abated as machines shut down.

Benjamin had returned from collecting a load of lumber. Ruth figured he was the one who'd shared the news of the occupant in the office. He'd have passed the buggies out front, recognized the bishop's and noted the unknown rig when he'd driven the team around the back of the shop. Her suspicion was confirmed when his voice carried across the now-quiet room. "Is he here?"

Ruth cleared her throat. "*Ja.* He's in the office talking with Bishop Weaver."

"What do you think?" The questions began as the men crossed to her.

I think that my life is about to change. But Ruth knew that wasn't what these men wanted to hear. "He seems a fair man." At least she hoped so. Impressions could be deceiving. Look at the one she'd certainly left him with.

"Does he know furniture?"

"I'm not sure about that. He looked like he was admiring the workmanship on that oak table and chairs you built, Isaac."

Some of the tension in their postures reduced with their laughter at her teasing.

"He knows that it's a *gut* business, that you do *gut* work and that we have many customers to keep us busy. He is not a fool." At least, she hoped not. "I'm sure he'll meet you soon." He would, or she would say something to him about making an effort to greet the anxious men.

Ruth smiled and gestured behind her. "You can go through the door to gawk and act like you've nothing better to do, or you can go back to work and demonstrate how industrious you are, should he poke his head into the workshop today."

The four men, two bearded, two not, nodded and turned back to their tasks. If she said it would be all right, it would be all right. They trusted her judgment.

Ruth's smile faded as soon as their backs were turned. She felt the weight of that trust pressing down on her shoulders. Pressing her down into the floor until she felt like she was barefoot instead of wearing the sneakers that provided comfort for long hours on her feet. A trust she didn't know if she deserved, but one she would do her best to uphold.

If there was no one to support her, well, she was growing used to that.

Ruth wove through the benches, equipment and various works in progress, and came to a stop at the far reaches of the large room. Pressing her lips together to keep them from quivering, she quietly surveyed the rough pieces of oak neatly stacked in the corner. Another Amish proverb crept across her mind. *A man should not grieve over much, for that is a complaint against* Gott. She compressed her lips more tightly. Chalk it up to another way in which she was disappointing *Gott*, for she certainly was still grieving.

And what was over much? *Daed* had only been gone
a month. *Daed*, who'd been father, teacher and companion, had left a staggering void here at the shop and
in the now-echoing silence of the farmhouse they'd
shared. It might've been different if her father had remarried after her mother's death when Ruth was born.
But he hadn't, much to the disappointment of all the
available women in the district. Instead, he'd raised
numerous eyebrows rearing his daughter by himself.
It'd been just the two of them. And now that it was just
her, she still felt his loss like a missing limb.

It wasn't that she didn't have friends. Ruth enjoyed
visiting with the other single women at church and afterward every other Sunday. Or at least she had before
Daed got sick. But between covering for his work at
the shop, keeping up their household and caring for an
ill father, she hadn't had time to go to the social gath-
erings like quilting. As it'd meant more time with her
father, she couldn't regret the trade-off. Besides, now
that the new owner was here, she had all the time in
the world to join in those events, at least until she left.

Crossing to a cabinet, she snagged a fresh sanding
block. Ruth reached up to pull her safety glasses into
place from where they usually perched on the top of her
head, but her searching hand only tapped hair and her
kapp. As her hand dropped to her side, she wondered
where she might have left them. Vividly, it came back to
her. They were in the showroom, on the counter. Where
she'd set them before she knew who he was. When her
initial thought upon seeing the blond, broad-shouldered
stranger had been how attractive he was and that she
didn't want him seeing her in heavy plastic glasses.

Where he still might be, rightfully thinking that she was the Wicked Witch of the West from a book she'd read to her *daed* while he was sick. But she wasn't going to venture anywhere near the showroom right now.

Well, she'd sanded without glasses before. Ruth returned to the corner, pulled a stool to the nearby bench and reverently picked up a flat piece of the oak.

She closed her eyes. If she tried hard, she could still see her father's handling of the wood. It'd been the last thing he'd worked on before he died. Every year for Christmas, *Daed* would make her a piece of furniture. The rocker was to be this year's gift. He'd tried to work on it, tried to hurry when he knew his time was running out, but the illness overcame him. Whenever she wanted to feel close to her father, she worked on the rocker. With dismal results. Because anytime she tried, like now, unshed tears burned her eyes.

This would not do, especially today. Ruth reluctantly tucked the oak back with the other unfinished pieces and wiped her sleeve across her eyes. As she lowered her arm, she caught the movement of the door to the showroom opening. All eyes in the room focused on the man who stepped through. Ruth took a deep breath. Time to start a new approach and hope her previous one hadn't obliterated her coworkers' options. Another Amish proverb popped into her head. *A smile is a curve that can straighten out a lot of things.* If only it were that simple. But it was worth a try.

Normally, Malachi strove to avoid being the center of attention. *Emphatically* strove to avoid it. Today, he knew there was no possibility of evading scrutiny. He was new. He was unknown. And he had some control over their lives. Until that changed, his actions and presence would be closely watched.

Looking out over the well-ordered workroom, he briefly met the eyes of the occupants, nodding at them as his gaze swept over their locations. Four men. And her. The fierce bantam hen. The distance to where she stood at the back of the room didn't diminish the energy that almost vibrated from her.

Whereas the men immediately returned his acknowledgments, there was a heartbeat or two from when his eyes met hers and he nodded to when she returned the nod. Apparently she'd thought better of her initial greeting, because after another beat or two, a smile curved her lips. It didn't reach her green eyes as he knew it could, from her initial response in the showroom. But it was an effort at least, albeit one that looked more like a grimace. Malachi wondered if it covered gritted teeth.

Not something he intended to explore or address today. He'd come in at Ezekiel Weaver's invitation for an official meeting. Malachi didn't know why the bishop needed to make it so official when a simple visit at Malachi's new farm would have sufficed. Perhaps, in having such an obvious meeting at the business, the man was attempting to extend over the new owner some additional authority as the district's bishop. Perhaps it was to make a point to the old owner's daughter. The man surely had his reasons. Malachi wasn't going to pursue them. He would establish his own path.

He made his way into the workroom, stopping to review and admire some projects, inspect equipment and visit with his new employees. In their own way, the four men expressed their welcome and interest in working for him.

Jacob, one of the two single men, was the most talkative. He also introduced himself as a nearby neighbor. Benjamin, the other unmarried man, was quiet but quick with a nod or smile. His eyes were sharp, taking in everything without being obvious. Isaac and Nathaniel, the two married men, were congenial and accepting. All of them seemed very capable in their work. All seemed ready to give him a chance. Except her.

She didn't approach him and Malachi didn't go back to greet her. An omission that perhaps had been a mistake, he reflected, as he went down the steps to the patiently waiting gelding. *Ach.* He wasn't going to retrace his steps now. He'd already met her. The rest of the workforce was aware of that. If they wanted to speculate about what they might perceive as an exclusion, so be it. He couldn't control their thoughts. He hadn't meant anything by it.

Except, Malachi realized as he climbed into the buggy and lifted the reins, maybe he had. Maybe he'd been unconsciously indicating that he was now in charge. Malachi winced as he released the brake. That hadn't been his intent, either. He had no problem with unmarried women working. He'd worked with some back in Ohio. Most were very intelligent. He had sisters who were sharper than some of the men he'd worked with.

The truth of it, Malachi admitted as the clip-clop of the bay's hooves signaled a ground-eating trot back to what was now the Schrock farm, was that he wasn't prepared to face the buzz saw of energy that radiated from her. His lips quirked. To think he'd be intimidated by a slip of a woman whose *kapp* barely reached his chin. Malachi's gaze took in the surrounding countryside that rolled by, his countryside now.

Well, he'd learn how to deal with her, one way or another.

Chapter Three

Bess trotted down the road at her usual lackadaisical pace. Ruth couldn't summon the energy to urge the mare to go any faster. She was in no hurry to get home to an empty house where the only sounds other than what she created were cracks and groans as the old structure settled.

Jacob, Isaac, Nathaniel and Benjamin had been encouraged by the short visit with the new owner. The reins dropped farther into her lap as Ruth sighed. Malachi Schrock. She supposed she should start thinking of him by his name and not as "the new owner." He wouldn't always be the new owner. One day he'd just be "the owner."

And she'd be gone.

A black-and-white blur, accompanied by energetic yapping, darted into the road. Bess shied away from it, causing Ruth to smack herself in the chin as she jerked the reins up to regain control. Guiding an agitated Bess into a nearby field lane, she set the brake. Heart pounding, Ruth looked around to identify the problem. A border collie puppy bounced out from under the buggy and plopped his rump down a few feet from the buggy step. He looked up at Ruth with his pink tongue lolling out one side of his grinning mouth, one ear up and one down. His eyes above the black button nose sparkled, as if waiting for Ruth to respond to his actions. She couldn't help smiling.

Securing the reins, Ruth hurried down from the buggy and squatted next to the pup. He rested his front paws on her bent knees. The white tip at the end of his black tail wiggled on the gravel as he showed his appreciation for her attention.

"Oh, you sweetie." Picking up the pup, she cuddled him against her chest. His warm squirming weight fitted into her arms, and her empty heart, like a puzzle piece. Closing her eyes, Ruth hugged him and smiled as he licked her cheek. Her eyes popped open and both she and the pup turned their heads at the exasperated call from up the lane.

"There you are, you rascal. Are you all right, Ruth?" Hannah Lapp strode down the lane, a frown on her pretty face. "I'm so sorry. We can't seem to keep the little stinker inside. All the rest of the pups stay put, but this one must be some type of magician, because he keeps escaping. Much to the dismay of the chickens and the pigs and the goats, and basically everyone on the farm." She stopped beside Ruth, hands on her hips as she regarded the errant pup.

"I don't think he made a good first impression on Bess, but no harm's been done. In fact," Ruth added after tucking her chin against the pup's soft head, "he's just what I need right now."

Hannah eyed her quizzically.

"The new owner came in today." The words were mumbled into the top of the puppy's head but her best friend heard them.

"Oh, Ruth, I'm so sorry." Hannah placed a hand on Ruth's shoulder. "I know how hard that must've been for you." Ruth had shared her feelings about the loss of the business with Hannah yesterday after church.

"Certainly made it real. No going back now."

"It is *Gott*'s will. He'll take care of you. You just have to trust in Him."

The pup wiggled to get down. Ruth reluctantly let him out of her arms. Arms that immediately felt emptier than the release of the warm weight justified. She knew her friend was right. Hannah had always had the *gelassenheit* that Ruth knew she should be practicing. But she couldn't just let things be. She couldn't help doing what she could to make things turn out the way she thought they should.

Standing, Ruth wistfully watched the puppy explore the territory around the end of the lane, the white tip of his tail waving like a flag over his chubby ebony back. Here in the abnormally warm November afternoon, the tension of the day faded as she watched the inquisitive pup. She didn't look forward to entering an empty house, but at least she could do it with a more peaceful attitude than when she left work.

The pup wandered over to sniff at the buggy's wheels. After confirming that Bess was going to tolerate the small investigator, Ruth turned to Hannah to share a grin at the puppy's antics and found her friend eyeing her speculatively.

"I think you do need him."

"What?" Ruth tried to recall the last bits of their conversations. They'd been talking about *Gott*. Of course she needed *Gott*. Everyone needed *Gott*. That was a given and one Hannah wouldn't have bothered to voice. Before that they'd spoken of the new owner. Hannah couldn't be thinking that Ruth needed Malachi Schrock, could she? A vivid image of the first moment she saw Malachi popped into her head. Her heartbeat had jumped at the sight of his tall form and intelligent eyes. It'd quickened even more at the smile he'd sent her across the showroom floor. Then her stomach had dropped when he'd said his name.

"No, I don't need him." Ruth held her hands in front of her as if to ward off the traitorously tempting thought. "We might not get along at all."

"Oh, but I think you already do." Hannah nodded to Ruth's feet, where the puppy was nipping at her shoelaces.

"You mean the puppy?" Ruth stared blankly at the busy dog.

"Who did you think I meant?"

Ruth wasn't going to go there. "I never thought about adopting a puppy." She knelt and was immediately rewarded with the wash of the pup's tongue on her fingertips. A great longing washed over Ruth. She looked up at her friend. "Do you really mean it?"

Hannah laughed. "We don't raise them to keep them all. We'd be overrun."

Ruth wrapped her arms around the pup and stood up. Now that the idea was planted, she couldn't let it go. "I'll pay you what he's worth," she vowed, mentally wincing at the hit to her funds because she knew the value of the border collies the Lapps raised and sold.

"I think we can work something out. Right now the greater value to us is regaining the peace that he continually disturbs. We might pay you to take him off our hands." Hannah rubbed the panting puppy's head.

"When can I take him?"

Hannah raised her eyebrows as she considered the question. "I don't see any reason why you can't take him with you today. Socks has begun to wean them. Let me get you some of the food they've been started on so you'll have something for him to eat until you can get back into town. You're sure you want to do this? I didn't mean to talk you into something you're not ready for."

Ruth bent her cheek to touch the pup's head. He twisted in her arms to try to lick her. "I may not be ready, but I can't think of anything I want more right now."

Ruth settled the pup in her lap and waved to Hannah before picking up the reins. A hastily assembled puppy survival bag rested at her feet. Bess flicked her ears toward the buggy, questioning what the new passenger was doing there. Ruth smiled as she checked for traffic before backing out of the lane. *Let the old girl pout.* Ruth was as happy as she could remember being before her father had come home from seeing the *Englisch* doctors and confirmed what was making him feel weak and lose weight was the cancer they had both quietly feared it to be. The smile stayed on Ruth's lips, curving up self-mockingly at the corners when she felt a warm wet spot growing on her lap.

The pup didn't seem to mind, as he curled into a ball and fell asleep. Ruth clicked her tongue, urging Bess to increase her speed. For the first time in a long time, she was eager to get home. Even if it was to start teaching her new roommate a few basic rules.

"I think rules are going to come easier for you than for me," Ruth admitted later that evening. "You're smart, and you should be, as border collies are one of the most intelligent breeds. I'm just afraid I'm not smart enough, or disciplined enough, to teach you what you need to learn."

Perhaps it had been a mistake to get a puppy, particularly with her plans. But after spending the evening with him—feeding him, taking him out several times, setting up a bed and later having him rest at her feet while she knit—Ruth knew she couldn't bear to part with the pup and face an empty house again.

Ruth reintroduced him to the bed they'd made together. She sat beside him as he settled into it, stroking his soft head before she slipped away. Only moments after she'd settled into her own bed, the cries started.

The whimpering tore at her heart. Leaning over the edge of the bed, she saw two miniature white paws propped up against her mother's Wedding Ring quilt.

"You're supposed to be a working dog. You will be shunned by border collies everywhere for this unacceptable behavior. You won't be able to eat from their dish. Or share treats with them. Why, I'd even be surprised if they allowed you to join them in working the sheep." While lecturing him, she lifted him to join her on the quilt. The pup licked her fingers. Ruth giggled.

The sound and feeling of the long-absent action surprised her. Giggling again just because it felt good, she settled the pup on the bed. They both snuggled in, comforted by each other's presence.

Her nose was cold. The weather had obviously turned overnight. Ruth nestled deeper under the covers until a sensation swept over her that something was missing. Her eyes flew open. The pup! Quickly sitting up, she patted around the bed in the predawn dark to determine he wasn't on the quilt beside her. Swinging her feet out from under the covers, she gasped as they hit the cold floor. Lighting a lamp, she saw a puddle near the door. Apparently she hadn't woken up soon enough to suit the pup.

"How long have you been up, and what else am I going to find?" Her teeth chattered in the chilly air as she snagged her robe from the foot of the bed and shoved her arms into the sleeves.

Wide-awake now, Ruth foraged for an old towel. Locating one, she looked through the open door into the living area. Of course, the pup had found the knitting she'd set beside her chair and was doing battle. And winning. Ruth wondered how many stitches she'd lost in the confrontation.

Hearing her footfalls in the bedroom, the pup raced through the door to investigate, almost knocking Ruth over. He licked her bare toes that curled on the cold floor before they both went to inspect the puddle by the door.

"This is neither approved nor appreciated behavior," Ruth admonished as she cleaned it up with the towel.

"*Housebroken* does not mean the house gets broken." The pup chased the dangling ends of the cloth as it moved. Lifting him into her arms, she rested her cheek on his downy head.

"Do you need to go outside so we can get the rules sorted out?" Slipping into her shoes, she glanced out the window to see patches of frost on the ground in the first faint fingers of light. Snagging a cape from a peg by the door, she draped it around her shoulders and stepped out into the brisk morning. A hint of rose to the east heralded the sun's future appearance. It was pretty now but could mean a weather change before evening. Might be prudent to throw an extra blanket in the buggy just in case.

The pup squirmed to get down. Ruth released him, hoping it was a sign that he wanted to do his duty. Instead, it was a sign he wanted to explore the underside of the porch.

Shivering at the wind that blew against her bare legs, she followed the pup around the yard, stomping her feet against the hard ground to keep warm. The pup was in no hurry. Apparently all he'd needed to do this morning had been accomplished already.

"If you're not going to do your business, we might as well set up a place for you during the day. Besides, it will get us out of the wind." Ruth hurried to the henhouse, abandoned since it had become more efficient to buy eggs from their neighbor instead of raising a few chickens herself. The puppy bounded along behind her, eager to investigate new territory.

The farmstead had several outbuildings. A hog house, a corncrib, a shed for machinery. All unused since Ruth and her *daed* began spending so much time at the shop that it made more sense to trade and purchase goods than grow everything themselves.

The henhouse had been one of the last buildings to empty. As soon as she ducked inside the door, Ruth sighed at the immediate relief against the whipping wind. She cast a critical eye over the dimly lit interior. Thankfully, she'd cleaned it thoroughly after the last of the hens had gone. A few adjustments and a warm bed should make it a worthy daytime home for the pup.

Ruth regarded the small run outside, considering what could be quickly done to eliminate all potential escape routes. The weave of the fence was small enough that he couldn't get out, but not so big he could get stuck, so no adjustments needed there. The pup assisted the investigation by tugging on Ruth's untied shoestrings. She bent to secure them and gave him a rub on his head. "Hannah was right—you are a rascal." Gently cupping his muzzle, she met his happy eyes. "In fact, that might be a fitting name for you. I dub thee Rascal Fisher."

Releasing the newly christened pup, Ruth stood, setting her hands on her hips. "So, Rascal. I need to get some tools and fix that hole under the gate. Hannah said you were a magician at getting out. I wouldn't recommend that today, as it looks like the weather is going to turn and I won't be around to check on you."

Worrying her bottom lip between her teeth, Ruth debated taking the pup to Hannah's farmstead. "I don't want them to think I can't handle you. I know I can, but it will just take a little preparation. And you shared a shed and a run like this with your siblings and mother.

You should be all right." She worried her lip a little more. "I hope."

Turning to look for the pup, Ruth caught him in mid-squat. "Good boy! That's just what we needed. Let's go inside for some breakfast while we figure the rest of this out."

By the time she secured Rascal's shelter, Ruth was running late. Bess's reluctant pace didn't help. The mare kept ducking her head against the wind that was blowing in her face. The sky was piling gray in the west. Ruth urged the mare to hurry whenever Bess's feet started to drag. She knew Malachi was going to be at the shop today. In fact, he might already be there.

Bouncing on the seat helped Ruth expend nervous energy. More important, it helped keep her warm. She was grateful she'd remembered to bring along an extra quilt and glad she'd taken a moment to roll down the curtain doors of the buggy against the wind, but she was going to be late. She had never been late for work before. Ever. The others would be waiting for her to open the door.

She'd taken a moment to stop at the mailbox of her nearest neighbor and stick in a message, asking if they'd check on the pup during the day. They had two daughters who still attended school. Ruth was hoping the girls wouldn't mind the chance to play with a puppy. Providing, she amended with another uneasy glance at the sky, they did it earlier in the day before some weather hit.

When she and Bess swept into the shed behind the woodshop, several other horses nickered in greeting. Ruth counted the bays in the makeshift stalls and her heart sank. They were all here. Plus one. Hurriedly, she unharnessed a grouchy Bess, wiped her down and guiltily gave her a offering of extra hay.

Cheeks flushed with more embarrassment than cold, Ruth dashed in the door. The recalcitrant wind took the opportunity to blow a gust that jerked the door from her chilled hands and bang it hard against the wall. Hastily shutting it, she turned to find all eyes in the workshop looking in her direction.

There were four sets of eyes she knew well. Upon seeing her, they nodded and returned to their work. But two new workers regarded her curiously. They watched as Ruth made herself walk sedately over to the coatrack, remove her black cape and bonnet, and hang them with the other coats there. They continued to observe her as she crossed to the cabinet and removed the safety glasses that she'd retrieved from the showroom yesterday—after she was sure he'd left. Since they were younger versions of the blue-eyed, blond man who also regarded her steadily, she figured they were the brothers who had come to join what had been her *daed*'s business.

Ruth put on the glasses and turned to face the new owner. Some type of barrier seemed prudent before meeting his gaze. Malachi didn't say anything, just flicked a glance to the clock over her head and raised an eyebrow before returning his impassive blue eyes to her. Even in his silence, Ruth felt severely chastised.

Swinging around to avoid his penetrating gaze, she grabbed the first project she could put her hands on and set to work. Struggling because her palms were now sweaty—not a good combination with the work she was doing on the wood—she took a moment to calm herself.

She was never late. With or without her father there, she'd always been the first one to the shop and the last one to leave.

It didn't take long before the familiar sounds and smells of the workshop lulled Ruth into her version of peace. Surprisingly, the morning went fast. Malachi didn't come near her, although he worked and visited with the men. Every time someone entered the sales shop, he looked over at Ruth, who always stopped what she was doing and went to greet the potential customer.

Having forgotten her lunch at home and not wanting to leave the shop during that break as she'd arrived late, Ruth took advantage of the empty office off the showroom to eat an apple she'd left in there when she'd been the sole resident. Looking out through the observation window into the showroom and farther to the street, she could see snowflakes joining the whipping wind. Ruth shivered. What a change in a day, but that was Wisconsin weather.

Wiping her hands with a napkin after disposing of her apple, she sighed. He still hadn't spoken to her. She wasn't sure what that meant. He hadn't come by to check the work she was doing. Did that mean he trusted her, or did it mean that it wouldn't matter what she did, so he didn't care? It shouldn't matter to her, as she was leaving. But she liked to know—no, she *needed* to know—where she stood on things. Squaring her shoulders, she ran her hands down her apron. Well, if he didn't talk to her this afternoon, she'd go talk to him.

On her way back to her workstation, Ruth paused to observe the two brothers, who were preparing to bore bolt holes for the frame on an oak headboard. Malachi's siblings were a good-looking pair. *Like their brother*, she thought to herself. It said in the book of Samuel that man looks on the outward appearance, but *Gott* looks at the heart. The new owner's—Malachi's—heart was probably good, something she had yet to discover, but his appearance was…distracting. And she didn't need or want distractions. Not of that nature.

Absently watching the brothers work, she abruptly straightened. They might be good-looking, but they were boring the holes on the wrong side of the bed-post. Ruth strode over.

"They need to go on the other side."

The older one looked up from the drill he'd pressed against the wood and swiveled his head toward her. The younger one lifted his safety glasses to the top of his blond hair.

"What?" Their inquiry came at her in a duet.

"You're boring the holes on the wrong side of the post. This headboard has beveled panels on the side facing the mattress. If you bore the holes for the frame there—" she pointed to where the drill bit rested "—the design will be facing the back of the bed, probably pressed against a wall. Benjamin did too good a job on the panels' bevels to have them adorned with cobwebs against a wall."

The brothers looked at her as if she had two heads. Ruth put her hands on her hips. Didn't they have any women with brains in Ohio? Their gazes flicked behind her. Ruth didn't have to look to know who was approaching. She could tell by the tingling that moved up her neck. Malachi must be focusing his judgmental blue eyes on her again.

"What seems to be the issue?" he asked mildly, moving into her peripheral view. She didn't turn her head.

The older brother nodded toward her. "She says we're putting it on backward." His tone implied that she couldn't possibly know what she was talking about.

Other sounds of the workshop filled the room, but their little knot was silent as Malachi's encompassing gaze swept over the headboard. Sweat gathered between her shoulders.

"She's right."

"What?" the siblings echoed again.

"There's a design on the side opposite of where you're drilling. You'd have put it on backward. If you aren't going to use your two sets of eyes, at least check things twice before you drill. Or cut. Or anything else." He looked over at her. "Thanks for the catch, Ruth."

"Even though the business won't have my father's name on it anymore, I still want it to be thought of as having superior craftsmanship and service." Ruth started for the back of the shop. She stopped abruptly. Sweet words. A smile. She sighed heavily. *Oh,* Mammi, *how wise you were.* Head bowed, she strode back the way she came until brown shoes under blue cloth pants came into view. Tilting her chin up—way up, it seemed—she met his eyes. "Thank you for your support. I appreciate it. I…I didn't mean to be…snappish."

His gaze held hers. Ruth's heart thudded in quiet beats until he spoke. "I want the business to be successful and well respected, too." He paused, as if he was going to say more, but then he seemed to think better of it and just nodded.

Ruth took that as the end of the awkward situation,

turned on her heel and headed back to where she would attempt to lose herself in the wood. And to try not to worry about the business. Or the pup. Or—she glanced through the glass portion of the door at the increasing volume of whipped snow outside—the weather.

Chapter Four

Malachi's lip twitched as he watched the diminutive figure stride away. That had to have been hard for her, Miss Nothing-Good-About-Having-You-Here. But she'd done it. His eyes narrowed as he watched her expertly resume the project she'd been working on. He'd been talking with his new employees. To every query, the response was the same: "Ask Ruth. She'll know." Was there any part of the business the woman didn't have her hand in? He could tell from the tone of the unprompted responses that she was respected.

He hadn't talked with her this morning. She'd looked like a cornered badger when she'd come in late. If she thought she'd been snappish a moment ago, he was thankful he hadn't approached her then. From his conversations with the men, he'd determined that she was always the first to arrive. So something must've happened this morning. She seemed more straightforward than to slacken her efforts just because ownership had changed. The recent interaction showed she cared about the future of the business. The question remained, would she have a future in it?

"Who's she?"

Malachi turned to see his twenty-one-year-old brother watching Ruth as she assembled what appeared to be a small rolltop desk at the back of the workroom.

"The previous owner's daughter."

Samuel rolled his eyes. "Oh, no. Not one of those again."

Malachi allowed a small smile in commiseration of the sentiment. *"Ja."*

"She going to haunt your steps like the other one did?"

His eighteen-year-old brother, Gideon, joined the observation of the auburn-haired woman, who fortunately wasn't aware of the scrutiny. If she glanced up, the "cornered badger" look would return, complete with hisses and snarls, Malachi thought as his smile progressed to a one-sided grin. Actually, Malachi mused, the analogy fitted pretty well. Badgers were small in stature, protective, blunt and aggressive. Like someone he'd recently met.

"She's not as pretty as Leah."

Malachi's smile evaporated at Gideon's comment. Yes, with her blond hair and thick-lashed eyes, the daughter of his boss in Ohio had been very attractive. But for some reason, the comparison to Ruth seemed unfair.

"This one works here. It couldn't be much worse."

"Samuel, what could've been worse is if she hadn't caught your mistake and we created an error for a customer on our first day on the job. Or had to waste labor and materials to do it over." The younger men's eyes dropped before their brother's steady gaze.

"*Ja.* You're right about that."

"Is the quality of work something I need to be concerned about going forward?"

"*Nee.* If only to make sure that she doesn't catch us at it again." Samuel nodded toward the back of the room.

"*Gut.*" Malachi dropped a hand on each brother's shoulder. He was surprised at how muscular those shoulders had become as he gave them a brief, encouraging squeeze. "I'm glad you're with me on this adventure. It would've been harder to leave Ohio without you."

"You did the right thing." Gideon earned another squeeze with his support.

"Let's hope so." Malachi patted their backs before dropping his hands. "Let's get some work done today. Show that the Schrock brothers know their way around building furniture."

Work was accomplished, but it tapered off in efficiency as the intensity of the weather picked up. Malachi watched his employees repeatedly glance up at the encroaching darkness that dimmed the skylights, the primary source of light for the business. Or go to the window and look outside at the growing storm, usually with hands on their hips and a worried expression on their faces. All except his single female employee. She stayed at her task until he could determine the project was indeed a petite rolltop desk. With the ominous change in the weather, no one entered the showroom to distract her from the work.

It was past midafternoon when Malachi called to get their attention. He waited until the machines had been turned off and the hums and squeals of the equipment died down so they could hear him.

"We want to get the work done on time for our customers. In order to do that, we need to ensure that you are safe and sound to come in and do it. We have storms in Ohio, and I've heard that the Wisconsin ones can be quite fierce, as well. We're closing up early today so you can get home and check on your families and livestock before the storm gets worse."

Although nothing was said, Malachi could tell by the relaxation in the tense faces watching him that his new employees appreciated the early release. He wanted his workforce safe. He was also striving to establish trust as their leader. Working hard in the long run did not always mean working all the time.

The men didn't need further instructions. Workstations were quickly cleaned up and equipment and materials put away for the day. Malachi saw his brothers by the coatrack, outer gear on and obviously ready to go. He frowned. There was some work in the office he wanted to finish before he left today. Malachi walked toward them, intending to instruct them to wait a bit before they hitched up the buggy. One of his new employees, Jacob, a beardless young man with red hair, was visiting with them as he put on his coat and hat.

Practiced at reading Malachi's expressions, Samuel grimaced when he saw his brother's face. "*Ach*, you're not ready to go yet. How long must we stay?"

Before Malachi could open his mouth, Jacob spoke. "I live just a mile up the road from the old Yoder place.

The house with the corncrib by the end of the lane. You two could come home with me and he could pick you up on the way by."

Obviously pleased with the offer from Jacob, whose age appeared to fall between Malachi's and his brothers', Samuel and Gideon looked hopefully at Malachi. It seemed a reasonable solution and one where they would get to know their neighbors better. Malachi nodded. "I'll see you there later."

The young men eagerly headed for the door and pulled it open. They slapped a hand to their heads as the vicious wind threatened to blow their black hats off. Gideon, the last one through, struggled to pull the door shut behind him. It finally closed with a hard click.

Malachi turned to see Ruth, whose workstation was in direct line of the gust, looking at the closed door with wide eyes and arms hugging her shoulders. They were the only ones left in the room. Tools and delicate pieces of wood were neatly arranged about her. She'd still been working.

"Time to go." Malachi tipped his head toward the door that rattled against the gusting wind.

She turned back to her bench. "I was late getting here. I need to put my time in."

Stubborn woman. Malachi strode over to the partially assembled desk. "*Nee*, not today. I won't have it said that I let you freeze in a ditch on your way home from work." Green eyes turned to him and spoke clearly that he did not *let* her do anything. Fortunately, she was prudent enough not to voice the words. He held her gaze. Really, the woman didn't need any aid in freezing. The outdoor weather would probably be ambient temperature for her.

Finally, she nodded and efficiently began putting away her work. Picking up a few pieces of oak to hand to her, Malachi ran his fingers over the smooth finish. The surface felt like silk under his experienced fingertips. He ran his eyes over the intricate joints in the desk. It was amazing craftsmanship.

"Beautiful work." He handed her the wood.

Taking it apprehensively, she flicked a look up at his face, judging his sincerity. *"Denki."* The rest of the pieces were gathered up quickly, as if to indicate she didn't need his help.

Malachi raised his eyebrows. Apparently it had been a temporary truce. The badger had returned. He wove his way through the workshop, now empty and quiet, to the showroom door. At the door, he looked back at Ruth. Once he was out of her orbit, her efforts had slowed and she appeared to be working on the desk again. Malachi frowned and jerked the door open with more force than necessary. Stubborn woman, indeed.

Deciding the tasks he'd hoped to finish could wait for another day, Malachi grabbed his coat and hat from the office and secured the front door of the store. Ruth looked up as he reentered the workroom. She scowled and had the rest of her work put away by the time he reached her.

Malachi waited while she tugged on her cape and tied her bonnet. He was going to make sure she went out the door and headed home. He frowned at the thinness of her cape as he followed her black-clad figure to the door. "I'll help you harness your horse."

"I can do it myself. Besides, I have to go to the store first."

Malachi stopped in his tracks. "What? Conditions are dangerous out there. You need to get home." The exasperation that colored his tone was a stranger to him. It'd never been there before. "Whatever it is will wait."

"No, it won't. I have responsibilities."

"So do I. I'm responsible for making sure you get home safely." He was tired of talking to the back of her black bonnet. Fortunately—or unfortunately—she whipped around and he found himself facing blazing green eyes and what looked like a few freckles on the cheeks under the encompassing brim. A dainty chin tipped up toward him above the big black bow.

"No. You are not. I've been taking care of myself for some time now. I don't need you to take care of me on your first day here. I'm going to Piggly Wiggly before I head home." Turning to jerk open the door, she almost tumbled into the wall when the force of the wind hit the portal. Recovering quickly, she bent her slight frame against the gusts and headed down the street to where Malachi had learned the grocery store was located. Her figure soon disappeared in the whipping snow. Shaking his head, Malachi locked the door and headed for the shed. Stubborn woman, he muttered to himself again. Even a badger was wise enough to get out of a snowstorm.

Ruth didn't know what made her cheeks more red, the blasts of wind that threatened to steal her breath or embarrassment and self-disgust at her behavior. Another proverb came to mind as she ducked her head against the blowing snow. *It is better to give others a piece of your heart than a piece of your mind.* She felt the staccato beat of snow pelting the top of her bonnet, like it was trying to tap the reminder into her head. Well, he had enough pieces of her mind to put together a puzzle by now. A piece of her heart? That was an amusing thought, even beyond the fact that he'd surely been baptized by now, and was therefore remaining Amish. And she wouldn't be. Therefore, not even a splinter of her heart would be allowed to consider his direction.

Besides, there wasn't room in her heart and mind for anything right now beyond fretting over the safety and security of the puppy, something she'd been doing all day. Was she responsible enough in her care for him? Was he smart enough to stay out of the weather? Unlike his new owner?

That brought her back to the abrupt discussion at the workshop. As she and the new owner were leaving, she'd had the discomfiting realization that not only would she not be the one to open the shop every day, something she'd done for years, she'd also no longer be the one to close it up at the day's end. So she'd latched onto the one thing she knew she could handle in accountability, her own care. After the way she'd lashed out at his offer, worrying about herself might be the only thing she had left to do. She might not have to worry about a job anymore, and she wasn't ready to leave just yet. *Dear Lord, please help me keep my mouth shut.*

Exiting Piggly Wiggly a short time later, she was almost blown back into the sliding doors. Ruth looked beyond the grocery store's parking lot to where the road was no longer visible and sent up another fervent prayer. *Please, Lord, I hope it is Your will that Bess and I get safely home to the puppy. Please don't let my stubbornness affect the two animals in my care.*

The relief from the blocked wind when Ruth entered the shed housing the horses was indescribable. So was her surprise at seeing Bess almost harnessed. Ruth dropped her bags by the wheel of her buggy and raced over to help. Looking up at her approach, Malachi seemed to take in the snow-crusted cape and bonnet.

"Did you get your important shopping done?" There was a curtness in his voice she hadn't heard before. Ruth winced, knowing she deserved it.

"Ja," she said breathlessly, reaching under Bess to hand him the girth. Her chilled hand touched his and she jerked it back. He paused momentarily, as well. Bess stomped her foot, encouraging them to get on with it. Ruth hurriedly renewed her efforts, careful to keep her hands on her side of the mare. She didn't want to explore the feeling that'd shot up her arm at the touch of his cool fingers.

Lifting up the shafts of the buggy, she guided Bess between them. Malachi was doing the same to a bay gelding. Faster than her at connecting the straps and buckles that safely secured the horse to the buggy, he came around to her side to help her finish. When he saw she was almost ready, he picked up her dropped bags and moved to set them in the buggy, glancing in the open sacks as he did so.

"You went out in a blizzard to get a dog toy?"

Ruth hunched a shoulder. "I needed it." She didn't

look at him as she scrambled into the buggy. But she caught a glimpse of his face before she secured the door. He was not happy.

She gently slapped the reins against Bess's back. The mare needed no further encouragement to exit the shed. Ducking her head against the blowing snow, she started a brisk trot toward home.

No nudging required for the old girl tonight. Ruth tucked the blanket about her on the seat, glad once again that she'd remembered to throw it into the buggy this morning. The mare wanted to get home to a warm barn and hay. Ruth wanted to get home to make sure Rascal was warm and safe. Getting out of the elements herself seemed like a pretty good idea, as well.

Within moments, the brown back trotting in front of the buggy was splattered with white. Ruth stared apprehensively at the road in the rapidly dimming light of the late afternoon. It was hard to believe that she'd driven in with brown and a bit of green fringing the roadside. Now she was glad to even see the sides of the country road that they'd just turned onto. Hopefully Bess's judgment was better than her own at knowing where the road ended and the ditch began.

Ruth was thankful she wasn't attempting this in the dark. She supposed she had Malachi to thank for that. And for harnessing Bess so she could head home sooner. Ruth saw motion in the small rearview mirror that jutted out from the buggy's side. A bay and buggy had just turned down her road. Recognizing the rig as the one ready in the shed before she'd left, Ruth frowned. He should've gone straight at the intersection. Why was

Malachi following her home? It would take him at least five miles out of the way on a horrible night.

As the temperature dropped, the light dimmed and the howling wind rose further, Ruth became grateful for the companionship on the road. It was the only company she encountered on the long, cold trip. When the buggy lurched as Bess cut the corner short into the lane, Ruth was never more glad to see the building shapes that identified her farmstead in the swirling snow. She darted a look at the chicken coop as Bess pulled hard toward the big barn doors.

Ruth would've gasped when she partially rolled up the buggy door to slip out if the wind had allowed her enough air to do so. The driving snow stung her cheeks and tried to tug her bonnet from her head. To keep from tumbling ahead of its force, Ruth kept hold of the buggy and then of Bess as she worked her way to the doors that shook ominously in their frames.

Bracing herself for the jerk when she released the latch and the doors suddenly became kites, she almost fell in surprise when two arms reached in front of her to pull the lever back and opened the doors in a controlled, albeit jolting, manner. Securing her attention, Malachi waved her into his own buggy. Bess needed no further instruction, driver or no. As soon as the opening was wide enough, she swept inside. Ruth hustled into Malachi's buggy. Driving the gelding into the big barn as well, she was instantly enveloped in the smell of hay and livestock. Malachi wrestled the doors shut behind them.

The sudden break from the force of the driving snow was eerie, as was the wail of the wind as it attacked the barn's walls. Ruth wobbled her way down the buggy steps, more shaken from the ride than she cared to admit.

Bess bobbed her head. Ruth knew the mare. She was saying, "I got you here. Now get me my supper." That reminded Ruth of her other charge. Dashing to the side door of the barn, she wrenched it open. There was a brief, startled call from Malachi before the howl of the wind shut out every other sound. Bowing her head against the buffeting snow, she pushed her way to the henhouse. Her cold fingers were clumsy on the door latch. Biting a chilled lower lip, she worked the frozen bolt from the latch, flung open the door and stumbled in.

Chapter Five

For a few heart-stopping moments, she couldn't see. Then her eyes adjusted to the dim light and she located Rascal on the makeshift bed she'd made him that morning. He blinked his eyes open and stretched his miniature muzzle in a yawn, showing his pink tongue. She hastened over and swept him into her arms. Her heart finally slowed to normal for the first time all day as she nuzzled her cold nose into the top of his head. Waking quickly, Rascal licked the snow from her face.

Sufficiently certain of his well-being, Ruth tucked Rascal under her cape, took a deep breath and stepped outside. By half running, she managed to keep her feet under her in the blowing wind. She reached the side barn door and struggled with it with her one free hand. "Hang on, boy. It's going to go flying when it opens." Moments later, plastered against the door by the wind, she was losing hope when it jerked open, held by a firm arm that gave her just enough room to duck through to the relative quiet of the barn.

Rascal squirmed to get down. Ruth knelt and let him

loose, the puppy erupting from beneath her cape like a magician's trick. Once he had his bearings, he hurried to explore the enticing smells of the barn.

Ruth rose to face Malachi. To her relief, he was watching the dog. The tension that'd coiled in her shoulders over worries about Rascal and the nerve-racking drive home seeped away. Concerned she might not be able to stay upright without hanging on to something, she stepped over to Bess and continued the work of unharnessing the mare that her unexpected help had already started. Within seconds, she could see Malachi's impassive face and snow-spattered hat over the top of the mare as he aided her efforts.

"New?"

Ruth didn't ask what he meant. There had been so many new things in her life lately. Only one that had caused her to act more erratically than normal, though, and had just popped out from beneath her cape. "*Ja.* I adopted him last night."

Malachi grunted in acknowledgment as he unbuckled the harness from the horse collar before removing the leather harness from Bess's back. He gazed at Ruth with a questioning look and she pointed him toward the tack room. Grabbing a brush and rag from a shelf on the wall, she proceeded to wipe the damp mare down before leading her into her stall. Preliminary investigations complete, Rascal scampered over to help when Ruth set about feeding the mare. Having located the straw, Malachi scattered some additional bedding in Bess's stall for the cold night.

When Malachi stepped out of the stall and secured the gate, Rascal bounced over to make his acquaintance.

Malachi knelt to the wiggly black-and-white bundle and proved himself an experienced puppy petter, hitting all the important spots until Rascal rolled over, exposing his belly in ecstasy.

Malachi glanced up to meet Ruth's watching gaze. "He's a fine one," he acknowledged as his fingers gently rubbed the silky tummy. "I suppose he's worth a toy or two." He shot a smile at Ruth before returning his attention to the puppy.

For a second, Ruth found it hard to breathe. When she remembered how, she drew in a long one, inhaling with it the comfortable smells of the barn—hay, horses and leather. The elusive feeling of peace flitted just out of her reach. She tore her attention away from the beguiling sight of man and dog and glanced across the barn to find Malachi's gelding watching her hopefully.

She hurried over to the bay, grateful for the distraction. "Oh, you poor boy," she crooned, rubbing his damp neck. "Can I get something for him?" She could hear Malachi's movements behind her. A moment later, she saw his steady form beyond the edges of her bonnet's brim.

"The rental place called him Kip. He's been a fine horse. I'm going to keep him." He rubbed the gelding's neck on the opposite side. "No point in doing anything when we're going right back into the storm, because we can't stay."

"No, you definitely cannot." Their eyes met over Kip's lowered head. "But at least let me get him a small bit of oats to eat while I fix you a thermos of coffee and warm up a brick for your feet on the trip."

Malachi scratched the bay under the black forelock

for a moment. "I suppose some hot coffee wouldn't go amiss. I saw where the oats are stored. I'll slip his bridle off and feed him some while you get the coffee."

"I doubt he'll go anywhere, but there's a halter in the tack room if you want to use it." She headed for the barn door, glancing in his buggy's open door as she passed the vehicle. After a brief pause, she marched over to her buggy and pulled the quilt from its bench seat to toss it on the seat of Malachi's buggy.

"I see you don't have sense enough to keep blankets in your buggy in this type of weather."

Malachi buckled the halter and then the oat bag over Kip's head. "I've been doing a number of things over the past few days. Thinking about blankets hasn't been very high on the list."

She huffed. "Wisconsin weather will take a heavy toll on the unprepared."

He pulled her forgotten grocery bags from her buggy. "Unprepared? Like not having dog food when you have a dog?"

Ruth scooped up the puppy that trailed at her heels and crossed to Malachi, her hand outstretched for the bags. He shook his head and retained possession of them.

"I'll help you get to the house. With this wind and your small sizes, the two of you could end up in the next county."

Aware that he had a point, she didn't argue. They headed for the exit. Knowing she also owed him something more, she spoke to the wind-rattled door in front of her. "I...I want to thank you for going out of your way and following me home, even though I didn't need it."

"You're welcome." His voice was bland, but Ruth could hear a trace of smile in it. Her lips curved slightly in response as she prepared to face the gauntlet between them and the house.

Malachi held the jolting door in check as she, with the pup again under her cape, slipped through. Ruth started for the house while he secured the latch. Stumbling against the relentless wind, she would've fallen if a firm hand hadn't grasped her elbow and pulled her upright. With one hand holding her close against him and the other pressed hard against his hat, Malachi guided them to the house. Once in the shelter of the porch, the wind dropped abruptly, as did Malachi's hand.

Ruth tried not to miss its surprisingly comforting presence as she pushed open the unlocked door to the kitchen. Malachi paused in the doorway.

"Ach," Ruth exclaimed, waving him in as she set the pup down. "You can't stay, but you can at least come over the threshold." Needing no further encouragement, Malachi entered and shut the door behind him. The ample kitchen seemed suddenly closet-size. Ruth busied herself with lighting a burner on the gas stove to make the coffee. Malachi stomped snow off his work shoes and pants before moving to the fireplace and starting a fire to chase the noticeable chill from the room.

The homey scene created a surprising ache in Ruth. She spoke quickly to dispel its unaccustomed appeal.

"I'll fix a sandwich for you for your drive home. You'll have something to eat in case you get stuck in a ditch."

"I don't think starving would be my immediate issue, but that would be much appreciated." He made quick work at the fireplace and soon a small blaze lent additional light and heat to the cozy room.

After hanging up her cape and bonnet on a nearby hook, Ruth nudged a few bricks scattered in the fireplace closer to the flames. She grabbed the puppy before he could launch himself in to investigate. Malachi reached out a hand when she crossed back to the counter. After a brief hesitation, Ruth handed Rascal to him. The ache intensified.

"Anything that isn't something my brothers or I have prepared would be *wunderbar*. I'm liking Wisconsin, but there are things I miss about Ohio already, and my *mamm*'s meals are one of them."

"The way I heard it, all the women within a reasonable distance have brought over some food. The single women anyway." She kept her back to him as she cut thick slices of homemade bread.

"Ja." There was a smile in the deep voice. "We've had a few meals brought over."

Ruth took the knife to a leftover ham roast and cut equally thick slices. "I haven't quite learned how to cook for one yet. I suppose I could bring something over when the unmarried community finishes feeding you."

She heard a sound behind her. She wasn't sure if it was a cough or a laugh. "I'll keep that in mind," he responded.

Ruth got out a clean dish towel to wrap the sandwich

in. It was quiet for a moment. Then she heard him wander across the dining room.

"This is a fine piece." There was reverence in his voice. Ruth turned her head to see him stroking the side of a bird's-eye maple hutch with one hand while he gently held the grinning pup in the other.

She pivoted fully to face him and the piece. "*Ya. Daed* made that for me for Christmas last year," Her tone was more melancholy than she intended.

Malachi rubbed the ears of the puppy cradled in his arm. "It's beautiful. And I'm sorry for your loss."

"No, it's a *gut* memory. It's the last piece he made me. He'd make me a piece every year. They started out small but kept getting bigger. There's that stool, the bench, the table."

Malachi studied the pieces. "The superior craftsmanship of the maker is easily recognized. Your *daed* was talented indeed."

Ruth blinked against the tears that threatened at his sincere comments. "Upstairs is a dresser, a headboard. A hope chest. This year he was making me another piece. He wanted to finish it, but then illness overtook him. I've tried to work on it, but it isn't the same. It was his project, not mine. Although I'd love to have it finished." She swung back to face the counter before she lost the battle and tears swept down her cheeks. "I'll figure it out somehow."

The coffee was boiling on the stove. Ruth turned in relief in its direction. Steam emanated from the openings as she filled a thermos she'd located in the cupboard. Gathering the thermos and the sandwich, she faced the room again to find Malachi watching her.

Their eyes met for a brief moment. She was the first to look away.

"Here, I'll trade you," Ruth said brusquely, handing him the sandwich and thermos and taking the pup into her arms, careful not to touch Malachi in the transition. "I'll go back out to the barn with you as soon as I feed him." She located the grocery bags Malachi had set down upon entering the kitchen and got out the small bag of puppy food. The sooner he left the better. His comfortable presence was creating a twinge of longing and that would never do with an Amish man, particularly one who was her new boss.

"No. You'll stay in here." Malachi was surprised at his adamant statement. He was less surprised at the indignant look she gave him in response. "I wouldn't trust that you'd be able to make it back to the house with the wind. You'd blow past my buggy and spook Kip. Then who'd take care of him?" he concluded, gesturing toward the pup.

Ruth nodded as she dampened the small amount of food she'd poured into a bowl. As soon as she set it down, Rascal squirmed in her arms to join it on the floor. Once there, he needed no encouragement to eat.

"And if it's this bad tomorrow, you stay home." Malachi tried to keep a straight face. He said it just to rile her.

"I will not!" She glared at him before marching to the fireplace. Using tongs, she efficiently pulled a brick from the fire. Wrapping it in a thick quilted cloth, she strode over to hand it to him. "But I will be prepared for the trip. More so than you were tonight."

Malachi pursed his lips and strolled over to the door. He'd won the battle he'd hoped to win.

"You better be safe going home. If anything happens to you because you helped me, I'll never forgive myself."

"I think you take too much upon yourself. It is *Gott* that forgives us," he said.

"That's true. Hmm. Then I'll never forgive you."

"But we're Amish. It's our nature and responsibility to forgive," he said. "Although you're a rather unusual one."

"Well, I'll think about it, then." She met his eyes, more than a hint of concern visible in the green depths. "Very hard. Just make sure you make it safely home."

"It will be *Gott*'s will, but I'll do my best. The gelding seems a decent sort. We'll get through."

"And don't get lost on the way there. You're new around here and the roads look different in the dark and snow." Ruth was looking out the kitchen window at the wind-whipped night beyond. She clasped her hands at her waist. The knuckles showed white in the tight grip.

"I've heard that. Somehow for twenty-four years, I've managed to make it home safely." Malachi waited until she moved her attention from the window to him. "Any reason you are so worried?"

She regarded him steadily for a moment. "The business would be up for sale again. You seem to know your way somewhat around furniture. It was extremely busy managing it alone and I have other things to work on. I don't want to have to do it again so soon." She almost smiled but managed to keep her expression solemn.

"I'll do my best not to put your brick, thermos and quilt into the ditch, or get them irrevocably lost in Wisconsin."

"See that you don't." Ruth admonished, bending to pick up the now-fed puppy to keep him from darting out when the door opened.

Malachi shifted the three items to one hand, pulled open the door and shut it firmly behind him when he stepped out on the porch. He grinned, feeling surprisingly warmer from her smile and concern than from the brick, whose heat was radiating through the thick cloth. The grin slowly faded as he took in the elements churning just off the edge of the porch.

The cold air stung his nose as he drew in a long breath. The barn was barely visible from the porch in the swirling snow. For sure and certain, it wouldn't be a pleasant ride home. Malachi wondered if the gelding would find his way to his more recent lodgings, or revert to a previous shelter and leave Malachi stranded outside the rental facility. He'd shrug if he weren't concerned his shoulders would freeze in that position. As he'd told Ruth, it was *Gott*'s will.

He descended the steps and bowed his head against the bite of the wind. It would be interesting if it was *Gott*'s will that he continue to ruffle the feathers of the bantam hen. The wind tried to blow him off course. Malachi glanced up, making sure he was still heading for the barn. He brushed by the fence of the abandoned chicken coop, recently converted to a puppy pen. No, Ruth wasn't a small hen; she was a badger, with many more defenses. Malachi had thought he'd left the foolish, adolescent desire to provoke a prickly creature long behind in his youth.

Apparently not.

Chapter Six

Ruth looked out the window until she could make out the gelding and buggy emerging from the barn. Malachi's figure was barely visible when he stepped out to wrestle the barn doors shut. She continued to watch as the buggy rolled out of the barnyard and down the lane, turning back to the kitchen when the lights on the buggy disappeared in the whirling snow.

"Well, Rascal," she said with a sigh as she regarded the pup in her arms. "We may have agreed not to escort him to the barn, but we still need to go out into the snow. You have some business to attend to outside. What do you think?"

Rascal licked her cheek, making Ruth smile. A laugh was beyond her reach when her mind was focused on the conditions Malachi was facing on his ride home. Bundling up against the weather, she took the pup out on the leeward side of the house. Unfettered gusts just a few feet from where she and the pup huddled whisked away the breath vapor that rose from her encouragement. Snatching him up before he began to run off and explore, Ruth hustled back into the warmth and safety of the kitchen.

Malachi was on her mind the rest of the evening. How useful one of the cell phones that young men sometimes carried during their *rumspringa* would be tonight. Malachi could call if he got into trouble or call when he got home safe. She would say thank you, and then what? She had no claim on him. She wouldn't be working with him for long. Certainly he'd seemed much more pleasant and fun than she'd anticipated. But he was probably pleasant to everyone.

Don't go there, Ruth, she admonished herself during the many times that evening she set down her knitting to get up and look out the window. *It is highly doubtful he's part of Gott's plans for you in that matter. You might work for him a bit longer, but for romance, you're crazy. You don't want to be an Amish wife. A wife, ja. An Amish one, nee.*

But after she'd settled the pup beside her on the quilt following their last trip outside for the evening, she closed her eyes. *Please, Gott, I pray that it is Your will to keep him safe.*

When she and Bess pulled into the furniture shop's buggy shed the next day, Kip swung his head their way and nickered to Bess before returning his attention to the hay net in front of him. Ruth tossed the quilt off her lap and scrambled out of the buggy to give the gelding an appreciative rub on the neck.

"Good boy," she crooned. "I'm so glad you got home safely last night." She returned to an impatient Bess, removed the harness from the mare and settled her into her own hay. The gelding was the only other horse in the shed so far. Passing Malachi's buggy on her way to the workshop door, she noted her loaned quilt folded neatly on the seat, with the dish towel, quilted cloth and brick stacked on top. Ruth smiled and left them there.

The day had dawned crisp and clear, as if to atone for yesterday's storm. The wind had finally stopped in the early hours, with four inches of snow covering the ground in a pristine blanket. Glad to discover the wind had kept the roads mostly clear and the drifts confined to the ditch, Ruth had no problem driving a grouchy Bess over them when she'd started for town earlier than normal.

She darted a look around the workroom as she entered. Her shoulders relaxed under her cape when she noted Malachi's two brothers, Samuel and Gideon, already at work. They looked up as she came in. She nodded in their direction, slipped off her bonnet and cape and headed to her station.

A few moments later the door to the store opened and Malachi came through. As she glanced up from assembling the pieces of the rolltop desk to meet his eyes, her cheeks heated. Quickly nodding in acknowledgment, she dropped her gaze back to the oak pieces in her hands. It took a moment before she recalled which piece went where.

It was easy to get into the groove of the assembly, though, when he ignored her for the rest of the day. They were quite busy for a day after a snowstorm, and the light and buzzer on top of the workshop door kept notifying her that potential customers had come into the showroom. But it didn't take long for Ruth to discover that not all shoppers were looking for furniture.

It being a relatively small district, the addition of three single men would prompt the young single women to come out, snow or no snow. Ruth thought initially that the first two women had actually come in to shop. They'd wandered among the furniture, touching a piece here, a piece there. Ruth had stood, smiling patiently by the counter, ready to answer any questions they might have or run up a sale on the manual addition machine that served as a cash register.

Some hours later, her smile was less patient. Ruth had learned by the end of the morning that any questions the day's customers had were all related to the Schrock brothers. The young ladies would meander around the furniture, but their eyes always drifted to the door to the workroom, obviously hoping that it would open and they could see through it or, better yet, someone would actually come through.

It made Ruth feel old. Most of the girls were younger than her, in their teens as opposed to her ripe old age of twenty-two. She knew who they were, but whereas their older, mostly married, sisters might be friends, these young ladies were more acquaintances. It also made her rather sheepish about her reaction to her time with Malachi last night. Was she as obvious in her interest as these girls were? She certainly hoped not. And her reaction hadn't been romantic. It had been more of a person finally having company in the house after an extended period by herself. That was all.

Ruth rolled her eyes when she left the workroom and went into the shop for the fifth time that morning and found Lydia Troyer, Jacob's sister, accompanied by another young woman. Both watching the door to the workroom with eager eyes. She almost smiled at their disappointed faces when she stepped through.

Although tempted to leave them alone in the shop to twitter away among the furniture, she took up her post by the counter. Any counter work she'd needed to do had long since been done that morning. There was nothing at risk in the store. Even though the young ladies were certainly strong and capable enough to haul out anything should they actually make a purchase— a doubtful prospect—they'd ask for help. And at least four, possibly five, single men in the back would be willing to lend it.

Ruth vowed that even if they purchased the massive oak rolltop desk in the corner, she'd maneuver it out the door by herself. Somehow.

At least Lydia came straight to the point. She had an edge in the apparent race. "Is Jacob here?" She smiled at her companion. "My mother wanted me to give him a message."

Jacob had been getting his hat and coat from the rack when she'd headed to the front to respond to the summons from the shop. "I think he was just going out the door to lunch." Ruth would have opened the door to the workroom to check, but it was apparent that was what they wanted her to do. Folding her arms, she resolutely kept her back to the closed door.

The young ladies obviously found this welcome news. There was only one café in town, so Jacob wouldn't be hard to find. And presumably, he hadn't gone to lunch alone. "We'll just catch up with him at the restaurant," chirped Lydia, and they scooted to the exit. "All three brothers were at my house last night," Ruth heard her say before they went out the door. "The two younger ones had supper with us and Malachi…" Whatever Malachi had done or not done was lost to the closing of the door.

Ruth hoped it hadn't been "and Malachi was frozen solid after following that stubborn woman home." Cringing, she equally hoped it hadn't been "and Malachi, once he got there, determined they should all stay the night," which would have been possible in the full Troyer household, but not at Ruth's, a single woman's home. Ruth sighed. Either way, it was none of her business. Especially as Malachi himself hadn't even seen fit to speak with her this morning.

She didn't put up the sign that she was out to lunch. Having gotten up quite early this morning—worrying through the night did that to a person—she'd packed a sandwich. As she stepped back into the workroom, her breath caught when she saw Malachi exiting the back door, also presumably to go eat. He stopped when he noticed her and their eyes held for a few heartbeats.

"I'll stay if you want me to." He stepped back into the shop and pulled the door shut behind him.

Ruth drew a shaky breath as she made shooing motions. "Go ahead. I'll be fine watching the shop. I brought my lunch. Go see how Miller's Creek survived the first snow of the season."

He hesitated, but nodded and left.

Ruth returned to the store, and through the large front windows watched him walk down the street toward the restaurant. She saw Lydia and her friend turn, smiles on their pretty faces, and wait for Malachi to join them in front of the café. Malachi opened the door for the women and the trio walked in together. Surprised at the hollowness that settled in her stomach at the sight—an emptiness not of hunger, but of an unexpected longing to join them—Ruth shook her head. She'd never longed for anything but taking effective care of the business before.

Her steps were slow when she entered the workroom and crossed to where her cape hung. Pulling a parcel out of one of its pockets, she eyed the ham sandwich ruefully. She unwrapped it and took a disinterested bite. She suspected it would have tasted a lot better last night, sitting on a cold buggy bench under a quilt in a snowstorm. With a certain somebody beside her.

The animated chatter of the younger people drifted over Malachi at lunch. He limited his contributions to a few nods here and there, although Jacob's sister, seated next to him, tried numerous times to bring him into the conversation. He just wanted to finish eating and get back to work. When he'd seen Ruth enter the workroom before he'd left, he'd been surprised by the hope that had risen that she'd ask him to stay. Instead he'd been shooed away like a fly at a picnic.

The woman was confusing. While his eyes had been peeled on the road last night, he'd thought about her— her warm brick at his feet and her quilt on his lap, even her sandwich in his stomach—throughout the journey to the Troyers'.

Samuel and Gideon hadn't said anything, but he could tell they'd been worried about his late arrival and were glad to see him. The Troyers had offered the Schrocks a place to sleep for the night, but as he'd come that far and their new farmstead was only a mile away, his brothers had quickly preceded him out the door and into the buggy. There had been no conversation that last mile. They'd anxiously watched for their lane in the blowing snow, trying to keep their teeth from chattering. His brothers didn't ask where the quilt had come from; they'd just squeezed into the front bench under it and pressed their feet close to the diminishing heat of the brick.

The tired gelding had earned the good rubbing and extra measure of grain provided him when they finally got into the big barn. Kip had definitely proven himself to be a keeper.

His brothers had been much more loquacious on the way in to work today. Enjoying the crisp clearness of the early morning and the snow-covered but travelable surroundings, Malachi had listened with half an ear as they discussed the rigs they wanted to buy. They'd sold their previous ones in Ohio.

"Kip is a good horse for you, Malachi, but I want something fast. And flashy. Jacob's brother knows someone who buys horses that don't make it on the track in Milwaukee, if you tell him what you're looking for," Samuel had enthused.

"Jacob said that Reuben Hershberger is the best place around for buggies. He usually has several used courting buggies on hand." Gideon was newer to the world of courting buggies but catching on fast.

Taking in the intricate drifts from last night's blowing snow in the passing ditches, Malachi had smiled as he listened. His brothers had been apprentices since they left school after eighth grade and had labored diligently since then. They had their own money. They would buy their own rigs, regardless of any comment he might make, although they might take any advice he offered into consideration. They also knew they would be working to buy hay this winter and putting up hay this summer to feed the new horses.

He hadn't been surprised when the conversation turned from courting buggies to potential girls to be courted.

"Accommodating of you to be so late last night, Malachi. It gave us a chance to get to know Jacob's family," Samuel had commented mildly.

"You mean it gave you a chance to talk with his sisters," Gideon had corrected. "Where were you anyway, Malachi? You were much later than we figured."

"I had something I needed to do." For some reason, Malachi didn't feel like sharing that he'd followed Ruth home to ensure her safety.

"Well, they are part of his family. A rather pretty part, I might add." Samuel had always been the most outgoing of the three. He would never hesitate to expand on an opportunity to talk with a pretty girl.

"You would." Gideon had always been comfortable being in Samuel's shadow. A comfort level that might change now that he was getting a little older and women were coming into the picture.

"Convenient there's three of them, although Lydia's the prettiest."

Malachi felt the sidelong glance Samuel had sent in his direction but he hadn't responded to his younger brother's teasing observation. He'd been more intent on getting safely home than noticing any women hovering around when he'd stepped briefly into the Troyer kitchen last night to collect his brothers. Any impression he'd had was that they were all too young for him. And he'd learned from previous experience that although pretty was pleasant to look upon across a kitchen table, it certainly wasn't the only, or even the most, important trait when looking for a wife. At least for him. Samuel would hopefully discover that for himself over time.

On seeing he wasn't going to get any response from his taciturn brother, Samuel had turned his attention to Gideon. "*Ach*, well, what we don't meet in the next week or so, we'll meet after church, Sunday after next. I'll have a buggy by then. I'll find a pretty girl to take home after singing."

"*Ja*. Only single girl we'll probably see till then is Ruth at work."

They had Malachi's full attention now. Kip flicked back his ears at the slight change in tension on the reins.

"*Ach*, she's too old anyway," Samuel said, dismissing their female coworker.

Malachi frowned. She wasn't that old. She was younger than his twenty-four years.

"Jacob said she'll probably go walking out with someone now that her father is gone. He said she ran the business as well as taking care of her father and the farmstead when he was sick. She said she didn't have much time for courting then. He figured that'd probably be changing now that the business has been sold."

Ruth had run the business while her father was sick? Malachi hadn't considered the possibility, but it made sense. Someone had to, and from what he'd heard, her father hadn't been in any condition to do so for some time. It would explain all the "ask Ruth" responses to any queries. It also made her attitude the first day he'd met her a little more understandable. He winced at the understatement. A lot more understandable. It was a good business. He wouldn't have wanted to sell it just because he was a daughter instead of a son.

Different districts had different rules regarding what was and wasn't allowed in the *Ordnung*. Apparently, ownership of that type of business by a single woman was verboten for the Miller's Creek Amish community.

On the heels of that thought, another thread from the conversation seeped in. Was Jacob Troyer interested in walking out with Ruth? There was a surprising twist in Malachi's stomach at the idea. He'd never had two employees who worked for him courting before. And if they got married, she'd have to leave. If they got married… Malachi didn't pursue the thought.

He didn't know yet what he was going to do about Ruth in the business. As far as operations went, particularly in light of what he'd just heard, she was an asset. The bookkeeping—far from Malachi's favorite part of the operation—was exceptional, and the recently added business, lucrative. Her coworkers' attitudes toward her were respectful, as well.

But women could be a distraction, whether they wanted to be or not. Leah had been. It'd been the primary reason that he'd left Ohio. And a business that used tools that could take off a man's finger or worse was not a place for distractions. He'd have to pay close attention. If there were any indications Ruth was going to be a distraction for the single men, now that she might be open to courting, she'd have to go.

Malachi suddenly became aware of the distant clatter of silverware and dishes around him in the restaurant, but an expectant silence at their own table. He looked over to see Lydia's gaze directed at him and realized he'd been asked a question by the young woman.

"I'm sorry, I didn't catch that."

Yes, a woman could be a distraction. But the girl beside him, avidly trying to get his attention, wasn't nearly as distracting as the thought that his female employee might be open to courting.

Chapter Seven

Winter descended upon Wisconsin. The next few weeks dropped a few more inches of snow on the ground, albeit more gently than before. Ruth made sure she and the puppy were up early, and she was urging a cranky Bess down the road with enough time to be one of the first ones to work. But she never arrived earlier than Malachi.

Ruth didn't know when he'd become just Malachi, and not the boss, or the new owner, but he had. What he hadn't done was pay her much attention, although Ruth would look up occasionally from where she'd be working and find his thoughtful gaze on her. Upon meeting her eyes, he'd usually nod and go about his business, but he never attempted to approach her.

Her father had set up the workshop so a craftsman would normally work a piece of furniture through all aspects of production. That way, they learned every necessary skill of furniture making. Also, if one worker was out for any reason, the work didn't pile up at his station waiting for his return. Granted, some workers were better at certain tasks than others. They'd assist those less skilled, particularly on intricate pieces, when needed. Ruth was relieved that Malachi hadn't changed the process. At least not yet. She thought she might lose some of the joy of woodworking if the operation became more of an assembly-line setup.

Ruth was also glad to discover the Schrock brothers were efficient and talented craftsmen. Malachi was particularly so. One of the many times she'd brought her lunch and stayed in the workroom, she'd strolled over to the project he'd been working on. It was a sideboard, which, instead of being part of a dining room set, was a stand-alone piece. She understood why as she examined the alluring design. Complicated yet sturdy, it personified its maker. Ruth had run her hand over the top, marveling at the smooth, glass-like finish. She knelt by the piece, examining the joints and details the average observer wouldn't notice. *Ja*, he was good. Perhaps not quite as good as her father, but very talented.

She wasn't surprised. From what she'd gotten to know of him, doing quiet, steady, yet beautiful work was consistent with his personality. Ruth realized he'd earned her respect, something she knew she was often miserly about granting. She still wished she hadn't had to relinquish the business, but for the first time, she acknowledged that it was pleasant not to have all the duties and concerns affiliated with owning and running a business on her shoulders.

Ruth could show up, do her work and go home. Granted, she was going home to an empty house with only a dog for company, but that could expand to visiting friends and neighbors as the weather got warmer and the daylight extended. But she'd probably be gone by then, Ruth reminded herself. Somewhere far away from the Amish community of Miller's Creek.

Instead of the peaceful sound of birds through the windows as they settled for the night, or the relaxing croaking of the bullfrogs in the nearby pond as she knit in the evenings, she might have a television. A radio would replace the charming occasional call and response of a barred owl, with their distinctive *who cooks for you*, as she worked a puzzle.

Because she wouldn't be on a farm. She'd be in a town or a city and hear none of those soothing sounds. It was what she'd always wanted, wasn't it? Taking a deep breath, she pushed to her feet. After one lingering finger stroked across the surface of the sideboard, she wandered back to her station and went to work.

Two days later, Ruth looked over to the door from her seat on the backless bench next to Hannah when the men started filing into the house, which the hosting Zook family had readied for church today. First the ministers and the older men walked in, then the younger married men, followed at last by the unmarried men and boys. There was silence where she sat among the single women, but she could feel the tense alertness as Malachi and his brothers shuffled by. Ruth pressed her lips together to keep from snorting. It was like a livestock sale, with potential buyers critically examining the new options that circled the arena. Well, there was no shopper more savvy for a bargain than an Amish woman.

Eyeing them critically herself, Ruth had to admit

the Schrock brothers were a good-looking bunch. No wonder they were causing a discernible stir among the unmarried women. Ruth speculated on how long they'd be able to stay single. Gideon, the youngest, had a few years yet to grow into himself, although he seemed a pleasant and hardworking young man from her limited interactions with him at the shop. She shook her head at Samuel, who'd had the audacity to wink in the direction of the young ladies. Ruth didn't envy the girl who'd try her hand at putting a yoke on that charmer.

And then there was Malachi. She watched as he took a seat, nodding to a few men he might not have met out in the barn where the menfolk gathered before the church service. Unlike Samuel, not once did his eyes stray toward the women. Ruth's mouth tipped slightly up at the corners. There was a lot to admire there. His vivid blue eyes, shared by his brothers, were approachable and steady. His shoulders under the black collarless jacket were broad and dependable. His hands, resting casually on his lap, were strong and capable. With only a limited number of families in the district, many with several daughters, any new unmarried men were regarded with a great deal of interest. Understandably, the unmarried ladies of Miller's Creek would pounce on him like dogs on a bone.

In fact, if she were looking for an Amish man, Ruth admitted to herself as she studied him further, she might look in that direction herself. With a heavy sigh, she turned toward the *vorsinger* as the song leader stepped forward to lead the congregation in the first hymn. But she was not looking for an Amish man. If she married, it would most likely be someone from the *Englisch* community. She'd marry into a lifestyle where she'd have freedom to learn more than her short years in education provided. To do things she was currently prevented from doing because of community constraints. To be more than what Plain living allowed for women. She'd made a promise to her father. Ruth swallowed against the lump in her throat as she tried to keep her face blank.

But that didn't mean she didn't enjoy Amish church Sundays.

It was something Ruth strove to remind herself of two hours later. The second preacher was giving his sermon. Ruth knew the man hadn't wanted the role as minister. He was a well-respected, hardworking dairyman who'd been nominated along with other men from the district. During the selection process, he'd picked the hymnbook with the scripture note hidden inside. The whole district had shared in his dismay. Because the man was obviously more suited to milking his cows on Sunday than leading the church service. And it'd probably be more interesting watching him do so than listening to him struggle through a sermon.

Ruth's wandering eyes fastened on movement on the benches where the unmarried men sat. Her coworker Benjamin's *bruder* was nodding off. She watched him sway ever further on the backless bench across from her. Her eyes widened as he teetered forward. Benjamin's countenance was expressionless, but his eyes danced with laughter as he shot out an arm to stop his eighteen-year-old brother from planting his face between the shoulder blades of the man seated in front of him.

Only the clasp of her hand over her mouth kept Ruth from laughing out loud. Her eyes, wide with merriment, briefly met Malachi's, where he sat straight backed, farther down the row. His well-shaped lips twitched before he returned his attention to the uncomfortable speaker.

A few hours later, Ruth shared the incident with Hannah as they poured coffee for the men when they gathered to eat. Hannah hadn't seen it, as she'd adhered to the church custom of not making eye contact with others during the service. But she joined in Ruth's laughter over the story. Later, when they sat down to eat after the men had finished, they speculated on who would be successful in winning over the Schrock brothers, a pursuit obviously being planned and executed by the young single women gathered in clusters around the room.

A few were already going out the door. Hannah and Ruth watched them from the kitchen window as the girls hurried across the buggy-track-rutted snow in the farmyard toward the barn, where the men had gathered to visit.

"They're going to freeze without their capes." Hannah's eyes were concerned under her furrowed brow.

"Oh, Hannah," Ruth scoffed. "They'd look like a flock of crows with their capes on and that's not how they want the single men to see them today. The barn is full of hay and men to flirt with. They'll stay warm enough."

"You're so cynical." Hannah's soft tone was more wry than chiding.

"I've seen them come into the shop often enough. And I've watched the maneuverings for other single men over the past few years."

"You should be joining in, not watching." It was a gentle admonishment.

"You know my thoughts on that."

"I was hoping you'd change your mind, with the business now sold."

"I think I'm even more set on leaving, now that the business is no longer mine." Her stomach twisted slightly at the memory of her promise to her *daed* to pursue her choice for her life.

"Has he been difficult to work for?"

Ruth didn't have to ask whom Hannah meant by *he*. "Actually, no. He's been pretty fair." Memories of the trip home in the snowstorm made her add, "And kind." More than kind, actually. He was funny, with a dry sense of humor. Hannah didn't need to know all these opinions, though. It might give her the idea that Ruth was interested in her new boss.

Her mouth went dry. She was a coward for not telling her best friend yet that she was leaving the community.

With relief on her part, they returned their attention to the window. The focus of their discussion was leaning against the fence of the dairy lot, talking with Isaiah Zook, the owner of the farm. Probably about cows. She'd heard Malachi mention to the men at work that he was interested in picking up a few head of dairy cows.

What he didn't seem interested in were the single women traipsing past him on their way to the barn. Or reappearing to pet the standardbreds in the lot nearby. Ruth scowled. Like they'd never seen a horse before. But no matter how much the young women flapped about the yard, Malachi didn't pay them any attention, remaining more absorbed in the cows and his discussion.

"Do you think he has a girl back in Ohio?"

Ruth blinked. It was possible. Some Amish young men didn't marry right away because they didn't have money or a job that could support a wife and family. That obviously wasn't the case with Malachi. He had the means, what with him buying the furniture shop.

Miller's Creek's single women were doing their best to attract his attention and it didn't seem to be working. Amish courtships were generally kept secret until the weddings were announced in church. Her eyes narrowed. Perhaps he'd come early to the community and his future bride was going to join him later, with a wedding soon to follow. She attributed the sudden odd feeling in her stomach to indulging in too many pickled beets at Sunday dinner.

"I don't know. Could be. But even if that isn't the case, Samuel seems interested enough for the both of them."

Hannah laughed in agreement as they watched Samuel, a girl on each arm, enter the barn.

A few other men, beardless and bearded, wandered over to join Malachi and the farm owner at the fence. Ruth saw Lydia Troyer, one of the capeless girls, approach the small knot of men. A few moments later Jacob's sister was at Malachi's elbow, his head bent in her direction. Ruth didn't know what was being said in the conversation, but she wouldn't be surprised if it didn't include a hint for a ride home later.

The surprisingly melancholy thought of Malachi taking Lydia home in his buggy prompted Ruth to remember her own need to head toward hers. She'd been tempted to let Rascal stay in the house alone while she was gone, but the idea was abruptly scrapped when she'd noticed a few tiny teeth marks on the bottom of one of her father's furniture pieces. Although she still felt guilty every time she left Rascal in the chicken coop with its accompanying yard, he seemed happy enough, and her furniture was safe for the moment. But she didn't like to leave him longer than was necessary. Especially when she felt like she abandoned him every day during the week.

"I need to harness Bess and get home." She'd already stayed much later than she'd intended. She'd forgotten how much she'd enjoyed the social aspect of church now that, as the business had fully changed hands, she wasn't the subject of as much discussion among her neighbors.

Or perhaps she still was. While pouring coffee at one of the long tables during the meal, she did hear some gossip linking her and Malachi's names, with no mention of furniture. The coffeepot had wobbled a little in her hand at the surprising thought of their names together. She'd steadied it with the reminder that having an Amish husband meant being an Amish wife. And that was no life for her.

As Ruth gathered her cape and bonnet and prepared to leave, Hannah reminded her, "Don't forget you agreed to come over to my *haus* for Thanksgiving."

Ruth promised that she wouldn't as she hugged her friend goodbye. In fact, she was thrilled with the invitation. It wasn't the first time the Lapp family had invited the Fishers to join them for a meal. But this was the first holiday after her father had passed. Ruth had dreaded the prospect of spending it alone.

Feeling warmer from the genuine farewells she'd received as she headed out the door than from the black cape that draped her shoulders, Ruth strode over the rutted farmyard to the barn. Blinking a bit in the barn's dim light after the brighter light of the fading winter afternoon sun, Ruth nodded to the male acquaintances gathered there. She made out Bess among the numerous bay horses and headed in the mare's direction.

With a smile, she shook off the offers from a few men to help her harness the mare. Ruth noted they'd all been eligible, unmarried men. She attended to the bad-tempered Bess. Farther down the row of horses, she could see Malachi doing the same thing with Kip.

Apparently Samuel had gotten his own horse, as he'd certainly be staying for the Sunday night singing. An activity that was actually more about ogling the opposite sex and allowing the young people to flirt than singing. But Malachi wasn't staying. Ruth quashed the errant, happy thought as she slapped Bess's hip when the mare cocked her rear foot menacingly. She finished harnessing the cranky bay, glancing up as Malachi led Kip out to where all the buggies were parked. Perhaps he did have a girl in Ohio. He didn't seem interested in exploring who was of marriageable age in Wisconsin.

As she exited the barn herself, she noted with glee that he wasn't taking Lydia home, either. Although the girl's eyes lingered on Malachi as he passed by her, she didn't leave the group of young people she was with to follow him out.

The snow in the unused pasture where the buggies were located was deeper than the much-traveled farmyard. Leading Bess across it, Ruth felt her shoes get wetter with every step. By the time she reached her buggy, her black stockings were soaked up to her ankles. Ruth grimaced. Even with the blanket she always carried in the winter, her feet were going to be freezing by the time she got home.

To keep from dwelling on her increasingly chilly feet as she maneuvered Bess between the shafts of the buggy, Ruth entertained herself with thoughts of summer footwear. She, like many Amish women and children, went barefoot as soon as possible once spring arrived. She couldn't do that in the furniture workroom because of potential hazards there, but she spent most of the season away from the shop barefoot. Ruth wiggled her toes in her wet socks as she imagined freshly cut, lush grass under her bare feet, or toes curling in the sun-warmed, loamy earth of her garden. A small smile worked its way to her face at the pleasant distraction when a voice from over the top of Bess's back jerked her to the chilly present.

"What are you smiling about?" Malachi regarded her quizzically as he attached the harness breeching to the shaft on Bess's right side.

"I was thinking about going barefoot."

"In this?" His eyebrow dubiously lifted as he took in the snowy landscape and the churned-up slush under their feet.

Her mouth twitched further at his expression. "Would it make you think I'm stranger than you already assume?"

"I don't think you're strange." He grinned as he ran the reins into the buggy through the opening in the windshield. "For all I know, you could be normal for Wisconsin people. Which frightens me." He ducked his head just in time to avoid the hastily made snowball, which splattered against his black hat and not his face.

Ruth watched warily as she hurriedly finished attaching the harness on her side, but he didn't retaliate. After banging his hat against his leg to knock off most of the snow, he replaced it and leaned against his side of Bess. The mare craned her head around to look at him and then shifted in Ruth's direction. Bringing Malachi's lopsided grin a step closer.

"You're not staying for the singing?"

"Does it look like I am?" Ruth forgot about cold feet as she met his amused blue eyes.

"Why not?"

"For one thing, I'm too old. For another, I know what I want and it's not in there." She nodded her head in direction of the barn where the single men were currently gathered.

His eyebrow rose again, touching the bottom of his blond bangs under the hat. "You don't look that old."

"I'm twenty-two," she announced pertly, knowing that her small stature made her appear younger.

"I stand corrected," he said, reaching up to flick a few crystals of slush from the shoulder of his black coat. "You don't *act* that old."

He had her there. "You provoked me."

"You provoke easily," he countered.

Ruth did. And she knew it. But she didn't have time to dwell on the fact or respond before he repeated a question.

"Why not?"

"Why not what?"

"Why are you not interested in anything in there?" He, too, nodded toward the barn.

Ruth didn't know if it was the cold or embarrassment that made her cheeks heat up. "Because they're Amish."

Both eyebrows rose into the blond fringe this time. "So are you."

"Maybe not forever." Bess stomped her hind leg and swished her tail, the long black strands barely missing Malachi. He leaned away from the mare and patted her on the hip as Ruth scrambled up into her buggy. She didn't remember to toss the available quilt over her lap as she guided Bess away from the other buggies and down the lane. She was plenty warm for other reasons. A glance in the rearview mirror revealed that Malachi stood there watching her departure for a moment before he strode over to the patiently waiting Kip and climbed into his own buggy.

Ruth smiled. Finally recalling her cold feet, she snagged the blanket and pulled it across her lap. She toed her shoes off and reached down to peel off her wet stockings before curling her feet up on the seat under the blanket. Ruth cast another look in the rearview to see Malachi turn out of the lane.

She sighed. There had to be a girl in Ohio. It was unusual that someone as attractive as Malachi was still single. A second sigh followed. As she had said, she wasn't looking for an Amish husband. And even if she was, she certainly wasn't going to fall for a man who already had a sweetheart.

Chapter Eight

Malachi was ready to get back to work by the time the Monday after Thanksgiving arrived. He'd been surprised at how much he'd missed his family in Ohio on the holiday. Adjusting to Wisconsin was easier and happier than he'd anticipated, but a letter from home made him nostalgic of past holidays there.

Thankfully *Mamm* hadn't mentioned Leah in her letter. It was more than he could say for his aunt Miriam, where the Schrock men had spent Thanksgiving. The Moses Lapps—no relation to Hannah's family— had been good friends of the Solomon Kings, so it wasn't surprising that his aunt mentioned Solomon's daughter a few times. Malachi just wished Aunt Miriam wouldn't look at him so meaningfully every time she said Leah's name.

But he'd been glad to be at his aunt's home rather than accept the other invitation they'd received from Jacob Troyer's family. Samuel had lobbied for that option until Malachi had given his brother a look and advised in no uncertain terms that they were spending

Thanksgiving with family. Samuel had wanted to go for the same reason Malachi hadn't: the Troyer daughters. Particularly Lydia. There'd been a lot of longing in that one's gaze, as well. And Malachi knew exactly what the red-haired girl intended.

Amish communities were relatively closed, with a limited number of families. Based on church last week, Malachi estimated this community to be around twenty families. That provided some but not numerous options when looking for a spouse. As a man with a well-established job, sometimes Malachi felt like he was hunted prey in a game preserve. He planned to marry someday, but he wanted it to be his choice. Not because he felt driven to it like a steer channeled through the barn until loaded for market.

So he was glad to be back at work. Where there was only one irksome woman to deal with. Although Samuel was finding her more irksome than Malachi this morning. Malachi observed the two preparing an eight-drawer dresser for shipment. Samuel was wrapping the piece in plastic to secure the drawers in place when Ruth stepped back to scrutinize the front of the dresser.

"The stain on those three drawers is a deeper red than the other ones." She pointed a slender finger at the ones in question. "I know we had another order for this set completed about the same time. Did we put three of the wrong drawers in this dresser?"

Samuel stopped wrapping plastic and looked at her, his normally charming smile absent from his face.

Ruth continued, her hands perched on her hips, "What does the other dresser look like? We haven't shipped it already, have we?"

Malachi watched as her diminutive figure strode to where Samuel indicated with a sullen tilt of his blond head. She critically examined the fortunately unwrapped dresser. "Yes. There they are. We need to pull those three and put them in the right dresser. How did that happen? We can't let this type of thing get out to our customers. What would they think of our commitment to quality workmanship?"

Watching his *bruder* assist her in switching out the drawers, Malachi covered his mouth to hide his smile. He couldn't disagree with her. Maybe he should think about letting his *bruder* go and keeping Ruth. He didn't know how the mix-up had happened, but the badger had ensured by her snarls and hisses that this would never happen again.

For sure and certain, it was not his style of management, but just as effective.

Malachi sighed as he looked at the numbers again and punched them into the manual adding machine one more time before documenting them in the ledger. He could do accounting, but it was his least favorite part of the business.

Tax work was done by an *Englisch* accountant, but there was still much that needed to be done at the shop. Ruth had done the majority of it the first few days after his arrival. Needing to be self-sufficient in that part of the operation, he'd taken it over. Sometimes you understood things better when you did it. Whether you did it well, that was another story.

The business was busy. He was fully cognizant of that. They were also making money—sometimes those things weren't synonymous—Malachi knew that, as well. Their success was due to the petite figure currently ringing up a sale to an *Englisch* couple at the counter. Her fingers were nimble on the counter's adding machine. Her smile and bright chatter charmed the customers.

He glanced at other ledger books under his elbow. She'd been nimble with the business, as well. Malachi knew Ruth had done most of the business management of Fisher Furniture, even before her father became ill. She'd done a good job. Malachi didn't know the exact numbers from Solomon King's operation in Ohio, but he knew enough to figure this business was more profitable. Because of the five-foot-nothing woman cheerfully escorting the *Englisch* couple to the door as she toted two child-size rocking chairs that'd just been purchased.

Malachi would've frowned at the *Englisch* husband for allowing Ruth to carry the chairs if the man's arms hadn't been full of two squirming *kinder* who'd presumably be using the chairs when they reached home. Ruth disappeared out the store door. She returned a few moments later, stomping the snow from her feet that she must've encountered when helping load the chairs in their car.

He watched her meander through the furniture in the shop, making slight adjustments to a piece here, sliding a chair farther under a dining table there. Malachi blinked when she stopped abruptly in front of a sideboard, wondering at her action until he realized that she would know every stick of furniture in the place and this was one he'd just put out that morning after he'd arrived. One he'd been working on when he found the time between bookwork and people management. She wouldn't have recognized it.

The hair on his forearm prickled as she reached out a hand to sweep it gently over the surface of the oak. Malachi swallowed hard at the action, almost feeling the sensation of her dainty fingers. Quickly looking away, he punched some numbers into the adding machine and scowled when he saw the results. He punched them in again before throwing down his pencil. When the same column of numbers came up two hundred dollars apart on separate calculations, he knew he was distracted. And being that distracted was no way to run a business.

The door to the workroom whisked open and drew the attention of them both. Samuel popped his head in.

"Hey, Ruth. You want to go to lunch with us?"

Ruth eyed him suspiciously. "Why?" she asked. Malachi didn't know if they'd interacted since the red-drawer incident.

Samuel's charming smile was in play. "It's lunchtime. And even though you're a tyrant, I'm assuming you still eat. Tyrants do eat, don't they? They'd have to keep up their strength, right?"

Sometimes Malachi wasn't sure if he liked his brother. This was one of those times. When Samuel looked at Ruth with a crooked grin and Ruth responded with a lopsided one of her own, Malachi decided he might be interested in some lunch, as well. He pushed his chair back from the desk and the onerous accounting.

"I've a feeling that in order to handle you, Samuel

Schrock, a person, tyrant or not, would need all the strength they could get."

"Well, come on, then." Samuel pushed the door open wider.

"I believe I'll join you." Malachi strode to the door of the office, just in case they forgot he was there.

Ruth's eyes flew in his direction and widened slightly. A moment later, she asked, "Does someone need to stay and watch the store?"

Two sets of eyes looked expectantly at Malachi. Malachi frowned. He was the boss. And he was going along, whether they liked it or not. He didn't fully trust Samuel not to put something in Ruth's food, or to try to charm her and put something in her head. Either way, they weren't going without him. "Put the closed sign up with a note saying we'll be back after lunch."

Ruth nodded and headed to the counter to grab the sign stating they were temporarily out that they used occasionally. Samuel looked in Malachi's direction and winked before disappearing back into the workshop. After some shuffling, Ruth found the note and scurried over to the door to put it up.

"You want to go out this way?" She nodded at the door beside her.

"Don't you want your cape?"

"The café's not that far. As long as you don't plod along, I won't get too cold."

Malachi fought against the urge to smile. He didn't want any comparisons to his brother's charismatic grin. Yes, plodding was his style, a pace with which Ruth wasn't acquainted. Just to prove he had other speeds as well, Malachi hastened to the door, opened it and gestured for her to precede him.

Although scraped free of snow, splotches of the sidewalk glistened in the noon sun. Ruth slipped on her first step beyond the door and shot out an arm to catch herself. Malachi quickly grasped under her elbow and steadied her. She cast a grateful look in his direction but didn't shake off the hand. It remained during their short walk down the street to the restaurant. Upon reaching the door to the café, she lifted her arm slightly. Not much, but just enough that Malachi let his hand drop to his side. He immediately missed the feel of crisp cotton and warm elbow under his fingertips.

A flood of sounds and smells engulfed them when Malachi opened the door to the café. After reheated casseroles and some not-so-successful experiences with his brothers' cooking, Malachi couldn't keep from enjoying the smell of roasted meat and baked goods.

Amish and *Englisch* alike filled the Dew Drop Inn, the din of their conversations a constant background noise. While the establishment had a few rooms to rent, the majority of their business came from its position as the only restaurant in Miller's Creek. The employees were primarily Amish but, owned by an *Englisch* couple, the café was open more hours than those of Amish businesses. The Dew Drop served Plain, family-style meals for the Amish and *Englisch* work crews that frequented the place. *Englisch* tourists seemed to think *family-style* and *Amish* were synonymous when it came to restaurants, but the eatery served burgers and fries, as well. Malachi's stomach growled as he eyed an overflowing platter of food.

Spying his brothers in the crowd, he motioned Ruth in that direction. Two seats remained at the table that included Samuel, Gideon, Jacob and Benjamin. Samuel looked up at their approach and indicated to Malachi to take the seat with its back to the wall, knowing that was where his older brother normally liked to sit. Malachi returned his nod. As he passed the other vacant chair, he noticed a small pile of melting snow on the seat. Shooting a disgusted look at his smirking brother, Malachi swiped it off the seat. Ruth paused beside the chair. Her eyes moved from the drops of water remaining on it to Samuel, seated across the table.

"Are we even?" she inquired mildly as she pulled napkins from the nearby dispenser and wiped up the remaining moisture before sitting down.

"*Ja.* But I want it known that I didn't mix up the dressers."

Ruth kept a steady gaze on him. "I understand, but regardless of who did it, we can't let something like that get out to the customer. It would've affected two different ones, and that's not something I'll allow out to represent Fisher—" she caught herself "—I mean *Schrock* Furniture." She darted a hasty glance at Malachi.

"I won't allow it, either." Malachi's tone was mild but decisive.

It was quiet at the table while Rebecca, the young Amish waitress, poured their water. She slipped away quietly when she finished without taking their orders.

"*Ach*, I think I may have done it." The admission came from a red-faced Jacob. "I worked on it the day of the storm and was thinking more about the weather than the work. It won't happen again, I promise." His glance at Malachi was earnest and concerned.

Malachi thought of the drive home in the snow that day and the interlude at Ruth's house. He nodded at the beardless man and Jacob relaxed. "*Ja*, that was an interesting day for many of us."

A subtly hovering Rebecca reappeared at the table to take their orders. Malachi wasn't surprised when she positioned herself at Samuel's elbow. They placed their orders one by one, and she whisked away, but not before sending a smile in his brother's direction. A smile that Samuel returned. Yes, his *bruder* was a flirt, but Malachi didn't mind, as long as he limited it to women who didn't work in the business.

"You are a marvel." Ruth shook her head after watching the exchange between Samuel and the waitress. "Have you met all the women of Miller's Creek yet?"

"Only the single ones," Samuel quipped. "Have I missed any, Benjamin?"

"If you have, I'm not going to tell you." Benjamin grinned. "I'm hoping you'll leave some for me."

"And me!" Gideon and Jacob both interjected simultaneously. Laughter rippled around the table.

"Do you need all of them?" Ruth furrowed her brow at Samuel when it died down.

"Not all. Just one…or two at a time. I like women. Why not shop when there's a marketful?"

"I like knitting, but I can only work on one project at a time without confusing the instructions. And if I bought all the yarn that intrigued me, my house would be overrun."

"I didn't say I was buying, only shopping." Samuel winked.

"If there's an instruction booklet that comes with women, I hope someone lets me know where to find one." Gideon's smile was a hesitant replica of Samuel's charming one. Ruth rolled her eyes. Samuel's next question had her blinking in confusion.

"How do you like cows?"

Ruth quipped, "Grilled medium well?"

"Don't we all," Samuel said, grinning his magical grin. "But my *bruder* here thinks they ought to remain on the hoof. And he must think we don't have enough to do already. He's bought a couple of dairy cows and a steer. We're going to bring them home this Saturday. You want to join us in the cattle drive?"

Ruth blamed her sudden light-headedness on hunger and the delicious smell wafting from the food just set on the table rather than the thought of being included in a family adventure. Particularly this family. Her eyes darted to a stoic-faced Malachi.

She liked livestock. Before the shop got so busy, she and her father had kept a few cattle on their farm. Ruth had fond memories of *Daed* teaching her to milk Bossie, the black-and-white Holstein they'd had. In fact, Ruth was beginning to miss having animals around now that she had a little more time. *Get used to it. You won't be able to keep any in a backyard in town. Better enjoy it while you can.* Casting another glance at Malachi, Ruth refused to identify what "it" might be.

"*Ja.* I'll join you." Suddenly, Ruth, who'd begun to dread nonchurch weekends, couldn't wait until Saturday. She enjoyed the banter of her coworkers during the rest of the meal. The easy conversation, Samuel's teasing of Jacob and Benjamin when they declined the invitation due to farmwork commitments of their own. It was *gut* to be part of a group. She'd missed it. She'd allowed herself to drift away from the closeness of the Amish community.

As she scooped up a forkful of mashed potatoes, the thought again popped into her head. *Better enjoy it now, because you won't have this kind of fellowship once you leave the Amish community.* Ruth put down her silverware. She was finding the last bite a little hard to swallow.

Chapter Nine

After getting a humpbacked Bess to hurry down the road in order to arrive at the Schrock farm on time, Ruth attributed her cold nose to the crisp Wisconsin winter morning. But her heated cheeks were due to the casserole dish she'd handed to Malachi when he greeted her after she set the brake on the buggy.

She felt sheepish about bringing food, but Ruth figured most of the district had already delivered basketfuls to the bachelor brothers. It was just being neighborly. Malachi handed the dish off to Gideon to take to the house as he returned his attention to harnessing the Belgians waiting patiently nearby in their fuzzy winter coats. The geldings looked like enormous stuffed animals that some of the stores catering to the *Englisch* carried.

"Thanks!" Gideon's smile was as bright as the sun just topping the eastern horizon. "Food deliveries have tapered off and none of us can cook. Fortunately, it picked up a bit after Sunday."

"I'll just bet it did," Ruth muttered as he disappeared

into the big white farmhouse. Remembering all the eager single women who'd eyed the Schrock brothers on Sunday, Ruth cringed that she'd joined the rush. She reminded herself the only reason she'd brought something over was because she'd told Malachi she would on the snowy night he'd followed her home. It wasn't like it was a cooking contest. So what if it was her favorite recipe? One her *daed* had often raved about after patting his stomach appreciatively. Didn't mean all men would.

Moving three head of cattle a few miles down the road from the Zook farm shouldn't take too long. Ruth secured Bess to the rail designed for that purpose and climbed aboard the back of the hay wagon, ignoring Malachi's outstretched hand offering assistance. The wagon shifted as he hopped on the end opposite from where she sat. It lurched forward when Samuel clicked the geldings into motion. Condensed breath drifted from the Belgians' nostrils and wafted over their blond manes. The wagon wheels crunched on the snow that had refrozen overnight as they rolled out of the farm-yard.

Ruth's fingers tightened on the edge of the wagon as it bumped down the lane. She turned her face to the east, absorbing the magic of the rising sun on a wintry landscape. It was going to be a beautiful day. They'd had a few days where temperatures hovered slightly above freezing, always a treasure in a Wisconsin winter. This looked to be another one. It helped keep the roads clear, but the ditches and glistening white fields beyond would be soggy beneath the surface.

The beauty of the morning didn't have anything to

do with the solid presence of the man whose feet dangled from the back of the wagon a few feet from hers. Or so Ruth told herself. Her hearing was tuned to that direction, but Malachi remained quiet.

Ruth forced her attention to the steadily diminishing view of the farmstead. Given the short time they'd been there and as busy as they'd been at the shop, the Schrock brothers had made significant improvements on the place. During his declining years Atlee Yoder had been stubborn and always refused community help. The place had fallen into disrepair. Evidence of the work Malachi and his brothers had done on the house, barn and pens adjacent to the barn was obvious. Come spring, when the ground softened enough to put in posts, they'd repair the dilapidated fences along the road. It'd be a beautiful place when they finished. Ruth sucked in some of the brisk morning air. Perhaps she'd drive by in a car later this summer. Just to see what they'd accomplished.

The wagon hit a bump, almost jolting Ruth from her perch. One of her boots nearly slipped off her dangling legs. She curled her toes in the black Wellington at the last moment, halting its downward slide. The boots were a half size too large, but they'd been the only size available at the store last spring. As she didn't have many outdoor chores anymore beyond taking care of Bess, Ruth figured she could make them work. The Wellingtons made sense for the morning's adventure, as she'd be walking through snow, mud and other things associated with cattle that she didn't want to step in with her good shoes. Ruth wished, though, that she'd put on two pairs of socks this morning, both to keep the boots on and for warmth. The frostiness of the morning was seeping through the rubber and her black knee-high stockings.

Ruth twisted her body to look ahead over the bobbing ears of the geldings. The dairy farm was in sight. A few miles' walk behind some cows would warm up her feet.

The Schrock brothers were quiet on the way over, seemingly as content as she was with their thoughts and the lovely morning. As they approached the lane, they outlined the plan for getting the cattle home. There were good fences, for the most part, on both sides of the road between the dairy farm and the Schrock place. One of the cows purchased was an older one, used to a halter. Samuel would drive the Belgians back, with that cow tied to the back of the wagon. The younger dairy cow and the steer purchased to fatten for meat should follow.

Gideon would ride with Samuel, hopping off to guard the corner on the one crossroad of the journey and the far side of the road once the wagon made the turn into the lane. She and Malachi would walk behind, keeping the entourage moving and addressing any traffic that might come upon them during the short trip. A little hay was loaded on the wagon as extra incentive for the cattle to follow. Cattle were herd animals. The younger ones should follow the cow led behind the wagon. There shouldn't be any issue.

Upon observing the new purchases in the lot, Ruth could tell the young cow wouldn't be a problem. She seemed docile and stayed close to the older Guernsey the dairy farmer was currently haltering. But the

shorthorn steer was another story. Ruth knew by looking at him that the roan would not be easy. Head up,
spooky-eyed and snorting in the chilly morning air,
he waited a few moments after the cows exited the pen
before dashing after them, kicking up frozen clods of
dirty snow behind him.

Ruth fell in step a cautionary distance behind him,
not too far back that she wouldn't have time to head
them off if necessary but not too close that the already-
nervous steer would bolt. The shorthorn would watch
warily a few moments as she and Malachi slowly ad-
vanced on him. Then he'd trot, head and tail high, to
keep up with the steadily moving cows before stopping
to watch and snort again. Half a mile down the road,
Ruth was already tired of his antics.

She began to think of him in terms of how she'd like
to see him cooked.

"Come on, Rib Eye. Just settle in there behind the
girls," she urged soothingly when the steer snorted,
spun and raced after the placidly plodding cows again.

"Easy there, Hamburger," she murmured as the
shorthorn spooked when he saw Gideon standing a
few yards down the opposing road when they turned
the corner.

"We're almost there, Chuck Roast," she encouraged
when he nosed the side of the road like he was thinking of checking out the ditch.

Malachi was quiet on his side of the road, content to
let her prompt the steer along. Ruth was very aware of
his solid presence and the slight smile touching his face.

While the Wellingtons were useful for doing chores
in sloppy conditions, they weren't so comfortable walk-

ing a few miles on a hard surface. Still, Ruth supposed she could handle walking the few miles between the farms if pioneer women could walk the hundreds of miles on the Oregon Trail, as she'd learned in school.

Ruth had liked school. She'd missed it for a while but had soon started working full-time for her father in the furniture shop. That was when the business really took off. With her father's encouragement and the previous bishop's approval, Ruth had taken some accounting correspondence courses. She'd set up their accounting system. Her fingers had itched to get on a computer, as some of their customers and other *Englisch* businesses had. Ruth's eyes flicked over to the man who walked steadily on the far side of the road. When she left the Amish community, a computer course was going to be the first class she took.

A startled holler from Malachi reminded Ruth she needed to focus on the present. Perhaps the spooky short-horn understood her nicknames and figured out what his destiny would be after a few months of fattening up. Or maybe the lure of the open field was too tempting. For whatever reason, Round Steak saw the possibility of freedom and made a dash for it. Just before the final turn into the lane, the roan-colored steer swished his tail, jumped into the ditch and was through a break in Atlee Yoder's dilapidated fence before Ruth could take the first jarring step down the steep decline.

She scrambled up the far side of the ditch, using tall grass that peeped above the snow to pull herself through. Ruth clambered over the downed fence, muttering as she went.

Dashing out into the snow-covered field, Ruth ran

at an angle to the steer to keep him from escaping into the woods that fringed the back part of the property. Gideon slipped over the fence behind the barn and hustled across the field to cut off the steer from that direction. The shorthorn stopped, snorting, head and tail up, before bolting to cut between them.

"Oh, you, Stew Meat," Ruth chuffed as she struggled to increase her speed across the rough field. Her boots were breaking through the recently frozen crust and getting mired in the muddier ground underneath.

"Hey!" she shouted, trying to distract the steer and send him back to the barnyard, where the docile cows waited. It wasn't working. Using one hand to hitch up her skirt, Ruth ran as fast as she could across the rough, snowy ground. Hitting another muddy patch, she stumbled when the boots didn't move as fast as her legs did. The shock of her stocking feet breaking through crusty snow had her shrieking in the next few steps but didn't stop her dash to head off the steer.

Ruth looked back to see her black Wellingtons sticking out of the field like short posts. The mud had sucked the loose boots right off her moving legs. Although her feet were colder, she was faster without the Wellingtons. As she ran, the field threatened to rob her of her socks, as well. Gideon increased his speed at her abbreviated scream. He and Ruth converged on the corner where the steer headed. The roan skidded to a halt. He looked at them warily before glancing back at the barnyard. Apparently thinking that he'd join the ladies after all, he turned and trotted toward where the cows waited, already in the pen, where Samuel had thankfully secured the older Guernsey.

Panting to catch her breath, Ruth scanned the field, looking for the black stumps of her boots. Now that the adventure was over, her feet, in wet and muddy stockings, were freezing. Hopping from one foot to the other as she tried to warm them, she figured she might as well hop like a rabbit back toward her boots. She cringed at the thought of cold wet feet in rubber boots on the long ride home.

She startled when a dark figure appeared beside her. Ruth's heartbeat slowed only slightly when she recognized Malachi, an unreadable expression on his face. He must have followed her, probably at a more sedate pace, across the field. Ruth couldn't imagine him scrambling up the ditch and running, coat flapping, across the field.

Ruth shrieked when Malachi swept her up into his arms and began walking across the field to the barnyard. Her heartbeat raced faster than the galloping steer as she felt his strong arms around her shoulders and under her knees. Hopefully he wouldn't feel it thumping against his chest. Hopefully he would think her breathlessness was from her race with the shorthorn and not from the sight of his beardless jaw just inches from her face. So close that she could lean just slightly forward and kiss him. If she so chose.

To keep from choosing to do so, Ruth curled her fingers into her palms until she could feel her nails cutting into the flesh. Wiggling for escape only caused the work-hardened arms to tighten.

"Put me down." Her command lost its impact when she could hardly find enough air to get the words out.

Malachi shook his head before dropping his chin to glance at her. "No."

Ruth's eyes widened. The drop of his chin put Malachi's well-shaped lips only a few inches from her own. Before she did something incredibly foolish, she turned her head toward the barnyard.

Her black bonnet had fallen during the run and hung by the bow still loosely tied under her chin. Fortunately her *kapp* was still secure, but Ruth could feel some pins coming loose. She could also feel the soft and steady thump of her head against Malachi's well-muscled shoulder with every step he took. Strange that the time it took to run to the corner of the field seemed a lot longer than the time it was taking to be carried back in Malachi's arms.

Samuel was standing by the pen gate, which, fortunately, the renegade steer had edged through. Ruth was surprised he hadn't spooked the shorthorn again as he was doubled over with laughter. Gideon, approaching from where he'd run to cut off the steer, looked like he was trying to suppress the mirth that'd taken over his *bruder*.

"Gideon, go get her boots," Malachi directed as he carried Ruth past.

As they approached the farmyard, Ruth's socks were getting icy from the combination of wet material and the winter wind that was kicking up. Otherwise, she was amazed at how warm she was in Malachi's arms. If she was getting frostbite, she wouldn't know it until she got home. And if she was, she currently didn't care.

When they finally reached the barn, Malachi shouldered open the gate from the field. "Samuel, quit your laughing and get that gate secured before you're the one chasing them all over."

Bess swung her head around as Malachi approached the buggy and set Ruth on the seat inside with her feet hanging out the door. Ruth sighed. She refused to interpret whether it was with relief or dismay that his arms were no longer around her.

"I don't suppose you brought other socks."

"I didn't think that I would need them." She could finally get words out, now that his lips weren't inches from hers. "What are you doing?"

"Looks pretty obvious to me. I'm taking off your wet socks before you catch a cold." Malachi looked up at her from under the black brim of his winter hat. His blue eyes glinted under his lashes. When had he gotten such long eyelashes?

"I need you healthy at work. We're having challenges filling orders in a timely manner as it is." Ruth got goose bumps when his warm fingers touched her knees. She had trouble hearing the rest of what he was saying. "Or were you really serious about this barefoot business you mentioned Sunday?"

"I try to limit that to the months of April through October." The chills that ran up her legs as he peeled down her muddy socks had nothing to do with the cold. "I can do that," she insisted, reaching down to push his hand away.

"So can I. And since you were kind enough to help me by driving cattle, I think I'll return the favor with the act of servitude by cleaning your feet." Ruth's heart thumped heavily as she looked down at his lopsided grin. How anyone could think that Samuel was the more charming brother, she didn't know. She exhaled a breath she wasn't aware of holding, relieved when Malachi turned his attention to his brother as Gideon dropped her black Wellingtons by the wheel of the buggy.

"Almost had to get a pair of pliers to pull them free." A smile still lit Gideon's face. "I washed them off at the hydrant."

"Thanks. Go into the house and get a towel and a pair of socks."

His younger brother looked surprised at the request. "Whose?"

"Doesn't matter. Any. If we have any clean ones," Malachi added drolly.

After dropping the soaked socks just inside the door of the buggy, he cupped her chilled feet in his warm hands.

Ruth almost slid off the leather seat. She searched for something, anything, to distract her from the enthralling sensation.

"So you can get them to bring food, but you can't get the single women to come over and do laundry yet?"

Malachi looked up from where he'd been examining her feet. "I'm not the one getting them to bring over food." He grinned. "But a clean load of laundry or two wouldn't go amiss." He returned his attention to where his thumbs rubbed slowly over the arches of her foot.

Ruth bit her tongue to keep from volunteering to march into the house barefoot to do laundry for him. She swallowed hard and quipped hoarsely, "You'll have to work on that."

"I suppose. But I'm not quite ready to let a woman

have free rein in the house yet. Some are like a spoiled horse. You give them a little and they'll take advantage and go where they want to go. Makes it pretty hard to get control back."

Samuel's head popped into view through the door of the buggy. He took in the sight of her feet in his brother's hand. "She gonna live?"

"*Ja*. Even walk again. But for the time being, she's going to be wearing a pair of our socks." Malachi turned at Gideon's approach and took the well-worn towel and worn but intact socks from his brother. He flipped the socks over his shoulder and used the towel to further warm Ruth's feet.

"How long did you have to search before you found socks without holes?" Samuel clapped a hand on his younger brother's shoulder.

"It's not any of yours, Samuel. It's hard to tell with yours which end the foot goes in—there are so many holes on the other end," Gideon retorted. "I brought a pair of Malachi's."

Ruth flushed at the thought of wearing Malachi's socks. Or maybe it was due to his hands gently tugging the dry socks up her now very warm feet and legs.

Malachi frowned when the socks slid back down her slender calves. After another attempt to secure them, he let them alone, much to her relief.

"You coming in to eat what you brought over?" Samuel nodded toward the house.

"Ah, no. I…I need to get back home. I left Rascal in the house as kind of a test. One I'm pretty sure he'll fail." It was as good an excuse as any. Ruth's normally tightly reined control was running amok, and unlike the recently herded beef, she didn't know if she'd be able to corral it before it escaped completely.

"You aren't avoiding it because there's something in there we should be concerned about, are you?"

"*Nee*, Samuel. Unlike you, I do unto others as I would have them do unto me," she retorted.

"It was only a little ice. Besides, it didn't work."

"That's because yours is only a little brain."

Samuel grinned at the comeback. "You'll do. Thanks for coming over and helping today, Ruth." He gave her a finger salute and tapped the edge of the buggy before turning to head for the house. Malachi watched his departure unsmilingly before returning his attention to Ruth.

"You always give folks tests you think they'll fail?" Malachi asked as he set her boots inside the buggy. Ruth smiled her appreciation, quickly pulled them on and swiveled on the seat to face the front. She didn't have an answer to that. Thankfully Gideon had untied Bess, which allowed her a hasty exit. She backed the mare away and headed down the lane with a parting wave.

Bess swung into a trot toward home, leaving Ruth free to ponder Malachi's question. Maybe she did give folks tests she expected them to fail. Was it a way of protecting herself? Somberly, she fingered the reins in her hands. If that was the case, then what kind of test would she unconsciously give Malachi?

Malachi watched Ruth's buggy turn right and roll down the road. Taking a deep breath, he headed for the barn. He tried telling himself it was to check on the

cattle, but Malachi knew it was to regain his equilib-
rium before entering the house and facing his surprisingly perceptive brothers.

He stepped through the recently repaired barn door.
The sweet aroma of alfalfa hay and clean livestock
greeted him. Malachi could see through the dust motes
dancing in the light let in by the midmorning sun that
the two cows had their heads buried in mangers of hay.
The roan steer jerked his head up from where he'd been
eating and eyed Malachi warily before chewing again.
Samuel had done a good job of settling them in. Malachi knew he would.

Good thing one of the Schrock brothers was thinking straight. Malachi hadn't since his heart had stopped
at Ruth's scream. Maybe it'd been more of a yelp, but
either way, it'd almost scared him out of his boots. He'd
been climbing over the downed fence when he'd heard
her shriek and was twenty yards into the field before
he saw what'd caused it and slowed his frantic run. All
he'd known was that Ruth was in distress.

Malachi exhaled slowly, the dust motes swirling in
front of him as he eased closer to check the cattle's bedding. Later, the distress had been his own. His mouth
grew dry as he recalled the feel of her slight form in his
arms and her dainty feet clasped in his work-calloused
hands.

He'd kissed a pretty girl or two in his twenty-four
years. He hadn't kissed Leah—that would've sealed his
fate—but he'd come close, since she'd been so available.
And pretty. But the thought of kissing the prettiest girl
in Knox County, Ohio, hadn't shaken him near as much
as the memory of the badger's surprisingly delicate foot

in his hand. Malachi jerked his felt hat from his now-sweating head. He'd have a hard time avoiding looking at her heavy black socks under the hem of her dress, now that he knew what was within them. Malachi jammed his hat back on his head in disgust, startling the steer, who whirled away from his hay.

"Easy there," Malachi crooned automatically, edging back down the alley of the barn. His lips twitched as he recalled the names Ruth had called the steer during the walk to the farm. He'd almost burst out laughing several times during the trip. Only his concern of scaring the animal had kept him from doing so.

Shaking his head as he climbed into the loft, Malachi wondered what was the matter with him. In Ohio, after church the unmarried men would fall all over Leah. Some would even come into the store on some excuse in order to talk with her. Malachi couldn't have cared less, even as Leah would look over at him with big eyes. But let one beardless fellow, most recently his *bruder*, interact with Ruth, and he got all riled up.

He climbed over some neatly stacked bales, glad the recently acquired Yoder barn was half-full of quality hay and straw. Making his way over to a small window, he unlatched its wooden door and pushed it open. Lying stretched before him was the acreage he'd purchased, and the gently rolling hills of the surrounding country-side beyond. Big white houses and big barns—some white, some red—dotted the landscape.

Enjoying the view, Malachi eased down onto a nearby bale. It was *gut* they had moved. Land in Ohio was expensive, and getting almost impossible to purchase with the growing Amish population there. Malachi still had two more brothers at home. Daniel, his youngest brother at fourteen, would inherit his father's farm, as was the Amish way. Due to the limited land, there was less and less opportunity to stay in farming, which was why many Amish young men turned to earning a living off the farm.

But farming was in his blood. So was helping take care of family. Malachi was hoping the farm and the furniture business would be successful enough that his other brother could join them. He knew Samuel and Gideon felt the same way. They might complain out loud, but they were familiar with hard work and didn't hesitate to tackle it. They'd eventually find their own ways. Thanks to the excellent management of a badger with surprisingly delicate feet, they had time to think about it. They were also in a position to have their next youngest brother, Wyatt, join them when their father was ready to let him go.

Malachi squinted into the distance, thinking about being ready. Several of his friends back in Ohio had already married. Beyond kissing girls, Malachi hadn't been tempted yet. He'd been too busy trying to establish himself at work, helping his parents watch out for his younger siblings and saving money to make a purchase such as the business and the farm. But now, he felt he was ready. For what, he wasn't quite sure. But as he rose from the hay bale and reached out to pull the Z-braced wooden door closed, he thought it might have something to do with an auburn-haired woman who didn't hesitate to run after cattle.

Chapter Ten

"*Ach*, you always make something with so many pieces." Benjamin was helping Ruth disassemble the petite rolltop desk. To confirm quality staining, they took the furniture apart to ensure the sprayed stain and sealant got into all the corners and small areas of the piece. After the staining and sealing processes, he'd help her wipe the sprayed pieces with a soft cloth to create a uniform appearance.

They'd partnered on this frequently over the years. Their actions were automatic, leaving time for easy conversation.

"Hannah said at church that you have a puppy from their dog's recent litter."

Ruth smiled at the thought of Rascal. The joy he'd brought to her life with his company and antics had been sorely missed. "Oh, yes. I'm struggling, though. There are things he could easily learn, if I just knew how to train him. And sometimes, when he does something and I know I should scold and make him behave, all I want to do is laugh."

Benjamin smiled in return as he unbolted a leg. "I know what you mean. We had a shepherd puppy one time. Smoky was his name. Smart as a whip. But with four young boys to see to his training…" He shook his head. "You can imagine how it went."

His smile extended further over his lean, tanned face until it was a face-splitting grin. "One time, my *brieder* and I were busy in the hog pen. I think we were sorting. The puppy tried to get in and help but just kept getting in the way, so we'd tell him to go. He did for a while. But he came back. With what he was apparently hoping was a gift." Benjamin snickered at the memory. Ruth poked him in the shoulder with a slat from the rolltop to get on with the story.

"*Mamm* had been hanging up the laundry on the other side of the house. While she was hanging up some sheets…" He started chuckling again. Grinning at his contagious amusement, Ruth poked him anew, highly curious by now.

"The puppy got into the laundry basket and pulled out some of her…" Benjamin blushed and waved his hand vaguely up and down in front of Ruth's torso. Ruth's eyes widened, not at Benjamin's gesture, but at the thought of a puppy running around the yard with Mrs. Raber's undergarments in his mouth.

"The puppy made it to the hog pen and before we could stop him, he'd crawled through the fence and started chasing the hogs with it. Waved it like a white flag, only he wasn't surrendering. Not his new prize anyway. And it didn't stay white for long. He wasn't very big or agile yet, and some hogs got by him, trampling on his prize in the process. Pretty soon it got mired in the mud, and with four boys and a puppy chasing hogs around a messy pen, it got lost." Benjamin attempted to get control of his mirth, only succeeding for a moment. "*Daed* found it in the hog pen three days later and offered it to *Mamm*. For some reason, she wouldn't wear it again. The puppy stayed chained up in the backyard on washday ever since." He burst out laughing at the memory.

Ruth started giggling and couldn't stop. It felt so good. Her eyes watered. She wrapped one arm over her stomach and covered her mouth with the other, trying to muffle her laughter.

Her merriment drew to an abrupt halt when she heard an exclamation from across the room where Malachi was working with a jigsaw. Turning, she watched him jerk a bloodied hand close to his chest.

It was good to be able to work on a few projects, Malachi reflected as he guided the jigsaw around a curve in the design. It was Thursday and the store was closed, but with so much business, his crew still toiled in the workshop. He was taking a welcome break from the office. The more involved he got in other parts of the business, the less time he spent actually making furniture. He missed it. Finishing the board length, he lifted it to examine the cut. Blowing off the sawdust, he reassured himself that he still had the knack.

As he eyed down the line of the walnut wood, he couldn't help noticing two of his employees interacting beyond it. He could tell from their faces and postures they were deep in conversation, apparently a particularly enjoyable one. He'd seen a lot of expressions flit across the badger's animated face, but so far, not one of total delight. At least not in his vicinity. It did something to her delicate features. Which did something to Malachi's pulse.

Narrowing his eyes on the couple, he set down the cut piece of walnut and picked up the next. They were obviously very comfortable with each other, her and Benjamin. Malachi checked the wood for the design he'd be cutting and inspected it for any knots or imperfections that would affect the cutting process. He grunted. *Comfortable* and *the badger* were not words he'd normally use together. Malachi started the jigsaw over the design, eyes down, but ears perked in the direction of his employees.

He was halfway through cutting the design when he heard a sound he couldn't identify. Malachi glanced up. The next second revealed what a terrible decision that was. He jerked his hand away from the saw. Then he identified the sound. It was Ruth. Laughing. Eyes brimming with mirth. Focused on another man. Malachi didn't have to think long at all to determine, for some reason, that he didn't like it. The focus. Not the merriment. The merriment was mesmerizing.

The pain in his hand intruded. Throbbed for attention, in fact. It was bloody. Malachi stopped and abandoned the jigsaw. Grabbing the bleeding hand with his right, he pulled it to his chest.

Closing his eyes, he tried to concentrate on how many fingers he gripped in his hand. Were there enough? He could feel the accelerated beat of his heart through the digits in his tight clasp. Sliding his right thumb to the end, he counted the tips. One, two, three and a very sore—but still there—four. Malachi blew out a breath he hadn't realized he was holding.

In two quick strides, he reached a stack of absorbent wipes they kept on hand for cleaning up stain and topcoat. Malachi snagged a few from the stack without letting go of his hand. Before he could loosen his fingers to apply them, small, cool and capable hands gently cupped his from underneath.

"Let me see," Ruth murmured. The demand was gentle but urgent.

Malachi loosened his grip. Immediately blood oozed from the end of his left index finger. Ruth quickly covered it with the wipes and reapplied pressure with her own fingers.

"Can you walk with me?"

"Ja." Sure he could. He could walk by himself. But he didn't want her to move from where she was, tucked almost against his chest, the back of her *kapp* almost brushing his chin. Malachi looked over the top of the *kapp* to see the men in the workshop converging on him if they weren't already hovering nearby. All eyes were concerned, particularly his brothers'.

"I'm fine. Just a little nick. Been doing too much paperwork and not enough woodwork."

There were a few beats of silence before Samuel spoke. "You'd better keep all your fingers so you can grip a pencil. Because none of us want to do the bookkeeping, either." The tone was casual. The speaker's eyes, not so much. Malachi gave an infinitesimal nod of appreciation to Samuel as the tension began to ease from the shoulders of the surrounding men with the resulting chuckles.

"I think he's just trying to get out of work," Gideon quipped, eyes wide with concern.

"*Ach*, that's more your line, little *bruder*."

"I learn from the best, *ja*?"

"Well. I suppose that is me, then." Malachi smiled over gritted teeth. His finger was throbbing. There was more laughter, then the men began to drift back to their own workstations. Malachi looked at his brothers. With uncharacteristic concern still in their eyes and characteristic shrugs, they returned to their work, as well.

He matched his steps to Ruth's as she eased him over to the sink and the cabinet above it that housed the first-aid kit.

She looked back over her shoulder to him, her expression apologetic. "It needs to be washed out in case there's any sawdust in it and then have antibiotic ointment applied."

Malachi nodded. He heard the words, but they could have been a chorus from the *Ausbund* for all he understood. Although he certainly wasn't thinking of the Amish hymnal. He was thinking about how beautiful she was.

Ruth turned back around and he was again facing the stiff muslin of her *kapp*. Malachi could see over the top of her head as she pulled down, one-handed, the first-aid kit, opened the metal container and removed the materials needed. She turned on the faucet and checked the temperature of the water. Carefully pulling the now-bloody wipe from his hand, she guided the hand under the water and quickly, carefully and efficiently washed it out. She then gently dabbed it dry with clean wipes before pressing a gauze pad against the wound.

Malachi winced a few times at the resulting sting of pain. He glanced around the workshop. Only a few brief looks were cast their way, and those came from his brothers. Malachi's lips quirked in another wince and stayed in a self-mocking half smile. Well, he now had Ruth's attention focused on him. Not intentionally, and not in a manner he'd have preferred. And she wasn't laughing. Malachi recalled the musical sound. Good thing he hadn't been working with the band saw or the table saw. He'd probably have cut off his finger, if not his whole hand.

Looking down at the slight figure before him, Malachi was glad her *kapp* didn't fully cover her ear. He could see most of the dainty shell that peeked out from its edges. There were so many delicate edges on the fierce little badger. She was like the desk she was finishing. Beautifully wrought, but sturdy and business-like. And time-consuming to properly appreciate.

Progress, particularly Malachi's, toward a satisfactory goal was measured in slow steps. He breathed in the scent of her hair that wafted through the *kapp*. Absorbing the warm clasp of her petite hand around his larger, rougher one, Malachi wondered what it would be like to be the focus of her joyful attention.

He speculated on the steps it would take to make that happen.

Ruth clamped the gauze against his finger, holding it in place while she waited and hoped the cut would soon clot. Looking down at the strong, tanned hand clasped in her smaller one, Ruth was startled to feel the hair follicles rise on her forearm. Her eyes swiveled from the goose bumps back to the clasped hands. It looked like they were holding hands.

A quick look while washing the wound had shown that, although currently bleeding steadily, the cut wasn't that long or deep. It shouldn't need stitches. She hoped. Ruth shuddered at the thought of what could have happened. Machines that cut and shaped wood could easily cut a man's hand. Malachi didn't seem the type not to pay close attention to what he was doing. She studied the calloused hand in hers. There weren't any white scars or healed abrasions that would've indicated previous accidents. That made sense with how methodical and careful he normally was. What happened today to affect his concentration?

She checked the gauze. Still bleeding. Sliding the finger of her other hand over his wrist, Ruth checked his heartbeat. Steady. Just like Malachi. She curled the wayward fingers back into her palm before they could stroke over the wrist with its light blond hairs. What was the matter with her? It was like she was the one light-headed from blood loss.

To distract herself, Ruth wondered if any blood had gotten on the project he was working on. If so, the stain should cover it. Walnut didn't come cheap. Of course, it came at a much lower cost than missing digits. Most of the blood covering his hand had come off when she irrigated the cut, but some red smudges were still visible. Ruth shuddered again, thinking of the missing fingers on some woodworkers she knew. He was lucky. He should have been paying attention.

"What were you thinking?" She didn't turn her head. Malachi was standing at her shoulder. Even with the renewed sounds of machinery starting up again after the scare, he'd be able to hear her.

There was a pause before he whispered, "I must not have been."

Ruth had never heard him whisper before. The surprising intimacy of his soft voice and the gentle wash of his breath by her ear raised gooseflesh on the back of her neck. Blinking her eyes at the sensation, she squeezed her fingers around his, only realizing her response when he flinched.

"Sorry." She quickly loosened her grip.

"'S all right," he murmured.

Ruth could feel the movement of his broad and steady chest with the brief words. She realized that if she closed her eyes, she could pretend that not just one, but both of his arms were around her again. And that his hand was entwined with hers not due to necessity but desire for her companionship. With Malachi, it could always be all right.

Ruth blinked her eyes open and the thought evaporated, leaving a feeling of longing as residue. Because she wasn't with Malachi. And never would be. She'd planned a different direction for her life, and marrying an Amish man wasn't part of it.

No, Malachi admitted, he hadn't been thinking, and he must not be thinking now. Because he was definitely feeling. And smelling. And seeing. Malachi tried to breathe shallowly, when all he wanted to do was take a deep breath to inhale the clean scent of what must be shampoo, as Amish women didn't wear perfume.

He felt the length of her arm against his, where they brushed from shoulders, along forearms, to meet at clasped hands. From his angle at her shoulder, he could see the sawdust sprinkled over the back of her delicate neck under her *kapp*, much like powdered sugar sprinkled over the top of a cake. No, he wasn't thinking when he blew a gentle breath over the surface, dislodging the golden particles until they floated in the air. The fragile strings of her *kapp* danced in the light breeze he created.

She jumped. Malachi winced, as she'd taken his hand with her on the ride.

"What are you doing?"

"You had sawdust on the back of your neck."

She huffed. "I probably always have sawdust on the back of my neck. Or stain on my fingers. At least it's better than blood." Her grip gentled as she checked the bandage again. Malachi was surprisingly content to let the cut continue bleeding. They'd barely studied any anatomy prior to finishing eighth grade years ago in Ohio, but from what he remembered, there was a good bit of blood in his body. He wouldn't mind a little more dripping out if it meant Ruth would keep holding his hand.

And it was definitely keeping her out of conversation with Benjamin. Malachi slanted a glance over to where the dark-haired man worked. Unlike Malachi, his attention was firmly focused on his work. Concentration was obvious on the clean-shaven face as he continued to disassemble the desk.

Apparently the flow had reduced to a trickle, as Ruth efficiently whisked off the bloody piece of gauze and replaced it with a clean pad. More gauze was wrapped around it to keep it tightly in place. In the process, the remaining fingers of his left hand were bound together. Malachi sighed as she slowly let go of his hand.

"Keep that on at least overnight. Tomorrow you might be able to get by with a butterfly bandage, topped by a large Band-Aid to keep it clean. I don't think you need to be in the workshop for the rest of the afternoon," she advised primly. "You seem to have enough issues working safely with two hands. We might have to call the *Englisch* ambulance if you try it with just one."

"*Ach*, I suppose you're right. I've got some work I need to look at in the office." It was his least favorite part of the business, the office work. Malachi was as comfortable as a duck on a pond in the workshop, with the equipment and managing the employees. But the office had been Solomon King's domain and Malachi had rarely ventured there. The office had been just off the store area, as this one was. The store had been Leah's territory. Malachi had avoided those areas as much as possible.

Ruth packed up the first-aid kit. Placing it back on the shelf, she glanced over at him. "Do you need some help?"

Malachi's heart thumped a little faster. Good thing the cut had clotted. "Probably. I'm trying to figure out your accounting system."

She scoffed. "It's easy. Didn't you look at the numbers before you bought the business?"

"*Ja*. But going over the profit and loss statements were easier than trying to read your chicken scratching."

"Ha. I'd imagine my penmanship is much better than what you've probably scribbled illegibly since then. I'd better go check to make sure it's something the accountant can read when she does the taxes." She marched toward the door between the workshop and store.

Malachi ambled slowly behind her. Suddenly, tackling office work didn't seem so irksome this afternoon.

Chapter Eleven

The following Wednesday afternoon, Ruth had half finished harnessing Bess before she noted the mare was grouchier than normal. Bess laid her ears back when Ruth buckled the girth. She rounded her back under the leather when Ruth swung her around in front of the buggy shafts.

"Are you sick?" Ruth stroked the neck of the cranky mare. Bess swung her head around and rubbed it against Ruth's shoulder, almost knocking her over. Ruth glanced at Bess's hay net. It was empty, so she'd had an appetite. Her water bucket was half-empty, indicating the mare had drunk normally during the day. A quick perusal revealed no signs of abnormal sweating in the chilly weather. Ruth rested her head against a harness-free area of the mare's belly, listening for sounds that might indicate colic. Everything seemed normal.

She couldn't ask any of the men what they might notice. She was the last to leave the shed that night, having walked to the Piggly Wiggly to get groceries after work. Since the day of his accident a week ago, she and

Malachi had been leaving work at the same time, but tonight he'd had to leave early to go to the lumberyard to arrange to pick up some lumber tomorrow morning.

Brow furrowed, Ruth climbed into the buggy, watching Bess carefully as the bay grudgingly trotted down the street. The mare was sluggish, but that was normal. The exception was that Ruth didn't hurry her as she normally did. Something was off. It wasn't until they turned the corner to head down their road that Ruth identified the problem. Bess was limping slightly on her left front leg.

Ruth winced as she eased the mare into a walk. It wasn't a bad limp, which was why she hadn't seen it at first, but the leg was definitely bothering the mare. There was nothing to do now but to get home in as comfortable a pace as possible for Bess. Ruth sighed. She had a good suspicion what the problem was. It didn't bode well for her, but taking care of Bess was the first priority.

It didn't take long to determine her hunch was correct. The harness was off, Rascal was investigating the corners of the barn and Bess was munching on hay when Ruth gently lifted the mare's hoof and rested it on her bent knee. After cleaning the interior, she carefully applied the hoof tester to the sole of Bess's hoof. The mare had a propensity for abscesses, the reason for the long-handled pincer in Ruth's grasp, and why she knew how to use it. She also knew to anticipate Bess's reaction when she found the spot of the abscess.

Ruth jumped back when the mare jerked her foot off Ruth's knee and snaked her head around with laid-back ears. Setting the tester out of the way, Ruth rubbed the mare's forehead. "I know it hurts, girl. I don't know why you get these so often." The situation arose at least twice a year. Bess ignored Ruth's sympathetic crooning and went back to eating, still with laid-back ears.

Frowning at the attitude, Ruth added, "I also don't know why I keep you." She picked up the tester and patted the mare's neck as she passed. "Must be your charm." Calling the puppy to her, she took the tool to the tack room and headed to the house for the supplies she knew would be needed. Her shoulders sagged as she went up the steps to the porch. It'd be close to two weeks before Bess would be capable of pulling the buggy. Foot issues for the mare meant Ruth was without transportation. For two weeks. In the winter.

It hadn't been an issue when her father was alive, Ruth reflected as she gathered iodine and cotton balls from the house. They'd just traveled together in his buggy behind Silas, her father's gelding. But after *Daed* died, she'd sold Silas and her father's buggy. Maybe she should get a pony cart and pony for times like these. But that'd be foolish. The smarter thing would be to sell the mare and get a more reliable horse. And there were means of transportation that didn't require a horse. If she left. Ruth swallowed hard. She meant *when* she left.

But for the time being, Ruth still had her crabby mare to deal with.

Bess had personality. And Ruth wasn't ready for another loss of someone in her life. Her father had purchased Bess when Ruth had started her *rumspringa*, giving his daughter increased independence in her late teen years. Selling the mare would mean losing a little more of her father from her life. With the recent loss of the business, she wasn't ready to do that. Even if it meant she'd be walking for the next few weeks in the frigid Wisconsin winter.

She treated the mare the way the repeated visits of the veterinarian had taught her. Opening and draining the abscess, then pouring iodine into the wound and stuffing it with cotton to keep it clean. A task to be done twice a day for a while to the thankless horse, although Ruth could tell the mare already felt relief. She'd pick up an equine painkiller tomorrow from the veterinarian when she walked into town.

Others would gladly give Ruth rides in the meantime, should she ask them. But she'd taken care of herself, her father and the business for so long that she shied away from the idea of depending on others if not absolutely necessary.

Ruth and the puppy went to bed early that night. The next few days would involve extremely early mornings to get everything done and walk to work on time. She'd been late once. She didn't want it to happen again.

Malachi finished unloading the new lumber and led Huck and Jeb to the shed for a well-earned rest. The load was heavier than Kip could pull so he'd driven the Belgians into town today to pick up the lumber from the sawmill. Pleased with the geldings, Malachi ran a hand down the fuzzy chestnut shoulder of Huck, the one closest to him. They were willing, strong and a well-adjusted pair. The other horses nickered as he led the big boys into the shed.

Absently glancing over at the other horses after he'd attended to the geldings' needs, Malachi frowned and ran another quick count. It was one horse shorter than normal. His brother's high-strung filly was there, watching him warily, as were the placid bays of the rest of his workforce. All were present except Bess. Ruth's mare was missing. A rapid scan revealed that her buggy was absent, as well.

Malachi narrowed his eyes. He knew she hadn't been in the workshop while he was unloading the wood. Because he'd looked. But he'd just assumed she'd been in the store during that time. Was she here today? Ruth never missed work. Was she sick? No one had commented on her absence. With a sudden urgency in his step, Malachi headed to the front of the shop.

Ruth looked over in surprise from where she was doing some bookwork at the counter when the door burst open with a wild jangle of chimes. Hoping his reddened cheeks would be attributed to the brisk weather outside, Malachi gave her a curt nod and strode through the store to the workshop door. He jerked open that door and stepped through, taking a deep, steadying breath as he did so.

After a brief glance to see who'd come through the door, the rest of his employees returned their focus to their work. Slowing his stride to a more leisurely pace, he walked to the rack to hang his coat and hat. His eyes touched on two of his employees as another possibility regarding the missing Bess surfaced. Had one of the single men given Ruth a ride to work?

He quickly eliminated Jacob. Ruth treated her redheaded coworker as a fond but exasperating brother. But Benjamin on the other hand... Their dark-haired coworker had earned a number of smiles. And rare, shared laughter, Malachi recalled, rubbing a thumb over the still-sore injury the laughter had caused him.

Shedding his coat, Malachi studied the broad back of his employee. He supposed a woman would find him attractive. Benjamin was certainly a good worker. Talented. Reliable. He'd be a good provider. He was pleasant. Had a sense of humor and an easy smile, which women seemed to like. Malachi turned and jabbed his hat on the peg hard enough that it dented the black felt. He really hoped Ruth hadn't ridden in with Benjamin. Ruth had said she wasn't interested in being courted by Amish men, but women changed their minds. They were always changing their minds.

The door to the shop opened and she came through. Moving over to the project he was working on, Malachi watched surreptitiously as she walked through the workshop to see if she paid any special attention to Benjamin. He frowned in confusion when the two didn't even look at each other.

"Everything all right?" Malachi almost jumped when Samuel spoke at his shoulder.

"*Ja.* Of course. Why do you ask?"

"You seem a little distracted, *bruder.* I don't normally see you like this. Is everything all right with the business?"

"The business is fine." Malachi's lips twisted. "Thanks to previous management, we have even more growth opportunities than I'd expected. The challenge may be in keeping up with all the orders."

Samuel gave him an odd look. "You don't look happy about it."

"I'm happy," Malachi muttered.

"Then what's the issue?"

"I'm not sure about the possibility of hiring more employees when I don't know if I can manage the ones I have now."

"You've never had a problem with employees before."

A small smile touched Malachi's lips in appreciation for the surprise and loyalty evident in Samuel's response. He focused on not letting his eyes slide to where Ruth turned on the belt sander. "Not until now," he agreed.

Malachi wondered all afternoon about Bess's whereabouts. Then he wondered why it bothered him so. He'd never spent so much time worrying about a horse. Ruth didn't speak with Benjamin that afternoon, or make any moves to hurry and get ready when the dark-haired young man left. When Ruth put on her cape and bonnet, Malachi was ready to go out the door behind her. To his surprise, she headed directly for the street, not the shed. Perhaps she'd ridden in with someone else in town? There was one way to find out.

"I didn't see Bess in the shed today." He fell into step beside her.

"*Ach*, she picked a fine time to have a hoof abscess. I'd rather she limit them to summer." Ruth looked up at him with a wry smile on her face. "More pleasant days for walking then."

Malachi halted, trying to absorb a strange sense of relief and the normal, growing feeling of exasperation he felt around this stubborn woman. "You walked to work today?"

"How was I to get here if I didn't?"

"That's several miles."

Ruth smiled tiredly. "*Ja*, my feet know it well." She looked in surprise at the hand he'd placed on her elbow.

"I'm giving you a ride home."

Her feet dragged a little as he pulled her gently along toward the shed. "No, you're not. It's miles out of your way."

"But Kip is used to covering miles. It won't be an issue for him."

"You brought Kip in to get the lumber from the sawmill this morning?"

No, he had not. He'd totally forgotten that in all his thinking about horses today. "Actually, no, I brought the team of Belgians." Malachi paused briefly at the realization and how it affected his sudden plans. It'd be a slow trip home with the geldings. But the prospect of that much time with Ruth didn't bother him. In fact, an unexpected sense of anticipation began to grow at the thought.

His eyes narrowed. He'd be late getting back to the farm after taking her home. Well after dark on the shortened winter days. Time wasn't the issue; it was the equipment. The heavier wagon was used for day work and didn't have lights that his buggy did. It could be a hazardous trip home in the dark with little visibility for *Englisch* drivers to see him. Hazardous for him and the geldings, too. Malachi frowned. He couldn't risk their safety. He remembered his recent inventory of the shed and smiled. The Belgians hadn't been the only Schrock horses in attendance.

"My *brieder* can take the geldings and I'll take you home in Samuel's buggy." Decision made, he continued to the shed. Ruth's slight weight was no obstacle to his firm but gentle hand under her arm.

She continued to drag her feet. "I don't know. Samuel may not let you. He seems pretty proud of that filly."

"He shouldn't be. She's a nuisance." Their coworkers looked up from where they were involved in various stages of harnessing their horses when Malachi and Ruth rounded the corner into the shed. Fortunately, Samuel was still there, adjusting the harness collar on the already-sweating filly. Malachi shook his head at the high-strung animal. A ride behind her wouldn't be relaxing, but it would get Ruth home, and both him and the Belgians off the road before dark.

"Wait here." He left her by Huck, a gentle giant of a horse. Ruth immediately started cooing to the draft gelding, rubbing the blaze on his face and running her fingers through the flaxen forelock. The big boy nodded his head in appreciation, almost lifting Ruth off the ground.

Malachi strode down the shed until he came to Samuel's filly. She jerked her head up, her eye ringed with white at his approach. Gently placing a hand on her croup on the opposite side from where Samuel was working, Malachi stroked her flinching flesh before he started helping harness the spooky animal.

"Easy, Belle," Samuel murmured to the filly as his questioning eyes met Malachi's over the tall brown back.

"Don't know why you call her Belle. According to the ownership papers that you left on the kitchen table, her name is Sour Grapes. At least one of those is correct. She's about as sour a horse as I've seen in a while."

"Don't pay him any mind, Belle. He's just jealous because you can run circles around his boring gelding."

"*Run* being the appropriate word. And if I had Kip here, I wouldn't be asking."

"Asking what?"

"Wonder if you and Gideon would take the geldings home and I drive Sour here."

Samuel blinked in surprise. "Why?"

"Ruth's mare has an abscessed hoof and she walked in. I'd drive her home with the geldings, but by the time I got home, it would be well after dark and the wagon doesn't have any lighting."

Casting an eye to where Ruth was now helping Gideon harness the Belgians, Samuel scrutinized her from beneath lowered lids for a moment. "You and Gideon could drive the geldings and I'll take Ruth home."

"No, you won't." Malachi was surprised at how fast and firm the words came out of his mouth. From the look on Samuel's face, so was he. Now Malachi was the one being scrutinized from under Samuel's lowered lids.

"No problem," Samuel finally agreed, a smirk on his lips as he shot a sidelong look at Ruth.

Benjamin was just finishing harnessing his bay mare next to them. The subtle sounds of the shed—the muffled stomping of hooves, the quiet snaps of buckles on harnesses, the faint murmurs of the men either to each other or to their animals—hadn't obscured their conversation. "I can give her a ride. I live in that direction."

"I got it." Usually Malachi appreciated the supportive nature of the Amish community, but for some reason, tonight the offers rankled. Benjamin shrugged and backed his mare from the shed. Samuel's smirk got wider. That rankled Malachi, as well.

"Anything I should know about Sour?" He prepared to back the nervous filly out to hook her up to Samuel's buggy.

The smirk transformed into a huge smile, showing most of his brother's white teeth. "She's not Kip," was the only advice offered as Samuel sauntered over to help with the Belgians.

Malachi snorted. No surprise there, he acknowledged, taking in the sweating neck of the filly again. They'd hardly left the shed. He eased the shafts down over her, attached the harness to the shafts, called to Ruth and stepped into the buggy. Looking around the unfamiliar interior of the rig and identifying the essentials, he recognized the used buggy as reflecting his brother's more outgoing personality. The bishop might discourage things that were *hochmut*, but either he granted leniency to the young men in their *rumspringa* on what might be considered proud, or the bishop had never stepped into one of their buggies.

The squeak of an opening door preceded Ruth's entry into the buggy, an enigmatic look on her face. She sat down, hugging the door, a good six inches between where her cape draped the seat and the edge of his coat. Malachi eyed the space between them before returning his attention to the filly. He pursed his lips. Between the two females with him on the trip, he wasn't sure which one would be more distracting.

Chapter Twelve

As the temperatures were above freezing, Malachi eschewed his gloves and stuffed them in his pockets. He wanted bare hands on the reins to keep a better feel for the unknown, and most likely fractious, horse. With Ruth seated on his left side, they sped down Miller's Creek's main thoroughfare. A glance in her direction revealed a smile on Ruth's face at the brisk pace they set. He had to admit, Sour Grapes was a smart goer. Malachi was beginning to see the allure of the filly. It wasn't long ago that he'd have wanted one just like her.

By the time they were out of town and approaching the corner where the intersecting road went to Ruth's farm, lather was already flecking off the filly's neck and chest. Sour Grapes kept jerking her head forward and playing with the bit. Malachi maintained a gentle hand on the reins. Approaching the corner, he slowed her down and put on the blinker in the buggy. She fought the shortened lines, tossing her head forward to pull more rein. She knew home wasn't that way and she didn't want to make the turn. Malachi's lip curled. How appropriate. The filly was already barn sour, wanting to get to her stall as soon as possible.

He battled her around the corner, keeping a close eye on the car behind him. Some *Englisch* drivers were very courteous in sharing the road with Amish buggies. Some were not. Malachi had a feeling the red car behind them might be one of the nots. Swinging wide on the corner, the buggy took up more than its normal share of the road. With a hard pull at the bit, Sour was speeding up. They completed the turn when, engine roaring, the red car honked loudly and accelerated down the road they'd just vacated. At the dual sounds, Sour shot forward at a gallop, every lunge jerking the buggy forward.

Malachi's hands tightened on the reins. He sucked in a breath as Sour headed close enough to the ditch that his side of the buggy tipped precariously in that direction. Malachi leaned hard the opposite way, banging shoulders with a bouncing Ruth. A powerful tug on the left-hand rein got Sour Grapes back on the road, where Malachi focused on stopping the bolting filly. Hopefully with the buggy and its occupants in one piece.

He knew, with the bit clamped in the filly's mouth, a steady pullback would do no good, so he began with alternating pulls and releases. There was no reduction in the horse's speed. At least they were more on the road now, although encroaching over the centerline. With the narrow bridge over the town's namesake getting closer with every lunge, Malachi figured this was a good thing. Or so he thought until he heard Ruth's gasp and looked ahead of the flying black mane to see a car approaching from the opposite direction.

Please, please don't honk, he beseeched the driver when it became evident they were going to meet on the bridge. Malachi's fingers clenched the reins and he gritted his teeth as the clatter of the shod hooves changed tenor when the filly's churning legs crossed the metal expansion joint from blacktop to bridge. The vehicle flashed by, the other driver's startled face only a few feet away. The car's protruding side mirror passed within a whisper of the buggy wheel.

Once they passed the bridge, the filly headed for the ditch again. The buggy tilted abruptly as the wheels on the ditch side left the blacktop. Harsh crunching sounds resonated through the buggy as they tore through fingers of snowdrifts that edged the road. Drifts that'd dwindled, but had been through numerous melt-and-refreeze cycles, causing the buggy to jerk in their direction at every impact. Even if it didn't tip, the buggy wouldn't hold up much longer with that kind of abuse. Wincing at the pain in his still-bandaged finger, Malachi pulled hard on the left rein, throwing the filly off balance and getting her back on the road.

Sour Grapes's chin tucked against her shoulder but her jaw was locked against the bit and she was still running. The buggy was rocking as she swerved, fighting for control. Malachi shot a glance ahead. The road was open. Taking a deep breath, he gave the filly a little more rein, letting her run. She'd eventually have to wind down.

Between alternate pulls on the right and left reins to keep her off balance and varying tugs and releases to slow her, he regained control. The filly eased into a trot and finally a walk. Malachi pulled her over to the nearest field entrance. The horse stood, lathered and quivering, as Malachi's hands slowly unclenched. Blowing hard, Sour Grapes extended her neck, demanding more rein.

Malachi gave her some, as what lay ahead of them was an open field with a foot of snow. She wouldn't get far if she took off again. He set the brake anyway. He was shaking. Not over fear for himself, but in terror that an accident could've hurt or killed Ruth. During the ordeal, his attention had been on the bolting filly. He'd been aware of Ruth bouncing and swaying on the seat beside him, but he hadn't been able to glance at her, much less give her any assurance, through the harrowing adventure.

The reins shifted in his hands, which were now sweating. Malachi shot an apprehensive glance at Sour Grapes, but she was just dropping her head to blow some more. She wasn't going anywhere. He could see Ruth's right arm, braced against the dash. Her fingers were white-knuckle in their grip. She was probably trembling with fear. Fear he could deal with. He'd pat her hand, reassure her that everything was all right now.

If she was crying... *Ach, nee.* He'd never dealt with a crying woman before. Not even his sisters. But any woman would deserve to cry over the past few minutes, even this little badger. Bracing himself with a few deep breaths, Malachi turned to face her.

Her bonnet was askew. The normally neat bow that tied under the stubborn little chin was undone, the tails trailing down the front of her cloak. Malachi had been partially right. The face that turned to him had wide eyes, but her green eyes were wide with excitement, not fear. They matched glowing cheeks and an open-mouthed smile.

Malachi couldn't help himself. He didn't even think about it. Leaving the reins in his right hand, he leaned over and cupped her cheek, gently holding her face still for the kiss he placed on her lips. Malachi's heartbeat quickly elevated beyond its rate during the wild buggy ride.

The leather reins moved in his hand. The buggy shifted as the filly took a step forward. Breaking the kiss, Malachi reluctantly leaned back, sliding his fingers away from the silken skin of her cheek. Ruth's eyes fluttered open and held his as he regarded her solemnly. He couldn't interpret what was behind them. No surprise there. He couldn't define anything in his brain, either, at the moment. Except that he wanted to kiss her again.

The buggy shifted once more. His mind whirling, Malachi adjusted the reins to both hands and released the brake. He looked over his shoulder to ensure traffic was clear and backed the filly, now willing, onto the road. The buggy rolled smoothly along as he clicked to the filly and she swept into an easy ground-covering trot. Malachi didn't feel the anxious vibe through the reins, so hopefully Sour Grapes wouldn't take them on any more misadventures on the ride home.

Sensing the horse was now on better behavior, he transferred the reins to his right hand. Reaching out, he took the graceful, yet deceptively strong one that rested on the seat beside him. After a brief hesitation, her fingers curled around his. They stayed that way for the remainder of the journey to her farmstead. No words were spoken, but his thumb rubbed gently over the smooth skin at the base of hers during the trip.

The filly slowed her gait when they turned into the unfamiliar lane. Malachi urged her toward the barn. As the buggy rolled to a halt, Ruth tugged her hand from his. It was with reluctance that he let go. Before he could set the brake, something he'd always do with this horse, Ruth opened the buggy door and scooted off the seat.

"Thanks for the ride." Her voice was a little breathless. She hastily stepped away from the buggy.

"Open the barn door."

"What?" Ruth's face, under the still-cockeyed bonnet, popped back in the opening.

"Open the barn door. I want to take a look at Bess's hoof."

"Oh, there's no need. I can do that."

"I know you can. I don't see a lot of abscesses and I want to see how it's treated." Lifting the reins, he shifted on the seat, tipping his head to stretch his back. "Besides, I'd like to get out from behind this *idioot* filly for a bit."

Ruth shot a look at the lathered, still, but currently white-eyed bay. A smile crept across her face. "I can understand that."

She hurried to the barn door and pushed it open. Malachi drove the filly through. Sour Grapes entered hesitantly into its dim interior until she heard a welcoming nicker from Bess. Malachi secured the reins, set the brake and stepped down from the buggy. Ruth had disappeared into the side room he knew held the tack and feed, as well as other equine essentials. Before he reached Bess's stall, where the cantankerous mare had her head out, ears laid back, Ruth returned with a hoof pick, cotton balls and a bottle of iodine.

Malachi held out his hand. A Band-Aid still covered his cut finger.

Ruth hesitated. "Are you sure?"

"I learn best by doing."

"You'll get the Band-Aid dirty."

"I'll put on a new one."

She frowned but placed the items in his hand. Opening Bess's stall door, she entered and held it for Malachi to follow her through before she closed it. "When you clean out the hoof—it shouldn't be too bad as she's been on straw for the day—you'll see where the plug is. Pull out the existing cotton ball, pour iodine in the hole and plug it with a clean cotton ball."

Malachi nodded as he stroked his free hand over the mare's neck and across her shoulder before sliding it down her front leg to pick up the hoof Ruth indicated.

"Be careful, she's cranky."

"Well, that seems to be the nature of all females who live on this property." Malachi positioned the hoof on his bent leg and applied the pick.

There was a muffled snort, followed by a brush against his shoulder as a slender hand reached out and lightly back-fisted him on it. Malachi smiled as he located where the cotton ball was wedged against the hoof wall.

"You seem to forget that we are a nonviolent community."

"You seem to keep provoking me."

Malachi deftly pulled out the cotton plug, filled the cavity with iodine before handing the open bottle to Ruth and secured the fresh cotton ball in place. Bess, apparently determining that his administrations were complete, or needed to be, snaked her head around with laid-back ears.

"Look out!"

Malachi jerked back at Ruth's warning, barely missing Bess's nipping teeth. Losing his balance in his crouched position, he knocked into a bent-over Ruth, who had been closely watching the proceedings. She fell under his greater weight, the iodine bottle, still open, flying against the wall. They both tumbled into the straw.

The fall knocked Ruth's much-maligned bonnet further askew. Malachi's startled glance took in her wide green eyes under the crooked brim. She was so captivating he was tempted to kiss her again. But the confusion in those green eyes and the restlessly shifting black rear legs of the mare in his peripheral vision stopped him. Malachi thought he might deserve a kick in the head for his wayward thoughts.

He levered himself carefully off Ruth and extended a hand to help her up. Casting a wary eye on the mare's hindquarters, she placed her hand in his. Malachi pulled gently, surprised at her slight weight when she gave the impression of such strength.

Her cheeks were flushed when she glanced his way before scurrying out of the stall ahead of him. With a respectful awareness of Bess's hind legs, he picked up the almost-empty iodine bottle and cap before exiting, as well.

Ruth had taken off the bonnet, readjusted her *kapp* and was retying bonnet ribbons when he reached her. She glanced up at his approach. Malachi capped the iodine bottle and set it on a nearby straw bale. Reaching out with a thumb, he brushed at the soft cheek now dotted with a few spatters of iodine.

"You've got a few extra freckles," he murmured as he leaned in, his hand moving to tip up the petite stubborn chin. His lips touched hers. Malachi's eyes drifted shut at the contact. Seconds later, they shot open when she jerked back.

"The puppy."

It took him a moment to identify the distant barking. He heard the incessant sound, punctuated with some frustrated yips and baby howls.

"I have to go."

Malachi easily interpreted the words not as "I have to go attend to the barking dog," but as "I need to step away from this." He nodded. He needed to leave as well, even though it was not what he wanted. Dropping his hand, he drew in a deep breath and stepped back.

Ruth self-consciously scrubbed her cheek with her fingers, making no impact on the additional orange dots. "I supposed we should be glad we weren't knocked into a pile of something worse. This might be harder to wash off, but it smells better."

Malachi smiled in response, knowing that was what she'd been hoping for.

She cocked her ear toward to the puppy's relentless barking. "I need to go check on Rascal." At his responding nod, she whirled and hurried to the big barn doors, shoving them open in an obvious invitation for

Sour and him to leave. Malachi didn't need to be asked more than twice. He climbed into the buggy, picked up the reins and released the brake. Fortunately, the filly was now in an amenable mood. She backed up like a champ and they whisked out of the barn. With a bemused smile and an attempt at a casual wave, Ruth sent them on their way.

Malachi clicked the filly into a brisk trot when they turned at the end of the lane. Sour Grapes seemed satisfied with the pace. Malachi almost wished the filly would bolt again. It would distract him from his now-galloping thoughts.

Ruth latched the barn doors and hustled to where Rascal waited in the repurposed chicken yard, miniature paws propped up against the wire fence. He'd ceased his barking once he'd gotten her attention and scampered over to greet her as she rushed through the gate. After sweeping him into her arms, Ruth nuzzled her nose into his warm neck.

"Thank you." She hadn't yet determined if the pup's intervention had warded off disaster, or spoiled a treasured moment. Rascal wiggled around to run his rough tongue over her cheek. Ruth doubted he'd have any success with the spots of iodine, either, but appreciated his assistance. She resolved to scrub her face frequently and thoroughly this evening. Not having a mirror—to have one might encourage vanity, and the Amish community had strong opinions against personal pride— she could only hope her efforts would be successful.

Stepping over the board under the gate that so far had kept Rascal from escaping, she set the pup on the ground. He followed her down the lane, staying in the ruts created by buggy wheels that wove through the melting and refreezing snow, as she went to collect the mail. While he scrambled along successfully, Ruth stumbled and almost fell more than a few times on the rough surface. Her mind was definitely not on the ground ahead. It was on the kisses. She drew in a deep breath of the chilly late-afternoon air, and only a small sense of self-preservation kept her eyes from drifting shut at the enticing memories.

The wild ride had made her heart race, but not as much as the feel of Malachi's lips on hers.

They had been more than she could've hoped for. As was the man. He was more…everything. Smiling dreamily, Ruth opened the mailbox door. Her smile faded. Ruth pulled out a large envelope, glancing without surprise at the return address. Her correspondence course had arrived, reminding her that her plans didn't include a husband—an Amish one anyway.

An Amish husband, at least in her district, meant her education would be over. It meant, once she had children, that working outside her home was over. Her responsibilities would be taking care of the home and *kinder*. She'd have no choice.

Ja, Ruth wanted a home, a husband and children, but she wanted other things, too, like *Englisch* women had. They had the ability to have a home and family without giving up other things they loved. It was what she'd desired since she'd reluctantly walked away from the one-room schoolhouse for the last time after graduating from eighth grade. Successfully absorbing more responsibilities at her father's business had only increased her resolve.

Her *daed* had known that. Which was why, before he died, he'd made her promise to pursue her choice. A choice he felt he hadn't had. With ambitions of being an engineer, Amos Fisher had planned on leaving the Amish community when he went to a Sunday night singing at the encouragement of some friends and fell in love with Naomi Schlabach, Ruth's *mamm*. As she was already baptized, he'd abandoned his aspirations and stayed, transitioning his dream of engineering into furniture making. They'd established a life in Miller's Creek. When she'd died during childbirth, he'd stayed, knowing the tight-knit community would provide much-needed support to a single father. But he'd nurtured Ruth's skills, encouraged her ambitions and pressed her to follow them, particularly when he'd realized he was leaving her.

It was the reason Ruth wasn't baptized. If she left before she officially joined the church, she could still visit and interact with friends and business associates in the community. If she was baptized into the church first and then decided to leave, she'd be shunned.

Ruth called to Rascal before he ventured any farther onto the road. She crossed her arms over the large envelope, holding it to her chest, and tried not to wish that her arms were instead wrapped around a strong blond man. She'd decided her future a while back, and it was not what was in the buggy she could barely see on the horizon, moving away from her.

Chapter Thirteen

"Ungrateful wretch," Ruth muttered, rubbing her upper arm after closing the stall door. Bess had taken advantage of her distraction this morning and nipped her arm. Ruth supposed she deserved it for not paying attention. *That will teach me. This is what happens when you don't stay on track. You get hurt.* She shot a baleful look at the mare, whose head was buried in the hay Ruth had provided before being bitten.

"You better enjoy that, you might not get anymore. In fact, maybe I will sell you before…" She paused and then went on, "Before I get some other form of transportation. You're not doing me any good now anyway." The pup barked and dashed in front of Ruth, almost tripping her up as he raced to the open barn door. She followed in his wake and looked out in the faint light of the sun, just hinted on the horizon.

A bay horse was trotting up the lane. A familiar one. Ruth's heart rate sped up and she drew in a shaky breath. *Remember what you decided last night.* The admonishment didn't do any good. A smile spread across her face as Kip drew to a halt in front of the barn.

"What are you doing here?" she asked as soon as Malachi pushed open the buggy's door.

"Making sure my employee arrives to work on time. We've got some orders to fill, as she keeps finding us more and more new business." Breath vapor floated away from the door as he poked his head out into the chilly morning.

Ruth didn't hesitate. "Let me put the puppy up and get my things." She called Rascal to her and they both bounced over to the chicken coop. Securing him for the day, she rushed to the house, closely monitoring the slick ground with her eyes and feet, but her mind wandered.

You're not looking for a husband! Her brain accused as she dashed through the kitchen door. *Yes, but that doesn't mean I shouldn't explore this*, she countered, grabbing her prepared lunch and changing from the Wellingtons to her work shoes. Her gaze fell on the kitchen table, covered with the correspondence course papers. Its allure was quickly supplanted by the memory of smiling blue eyes under a black felt hat. *Which one do you want to greet each morning?*

The ride into town was much less adventurous behind the sedate Kip instead of the unpredictable filly. Ruth kept her hands folded in her lap on the journey, afraid if she draped the right one casually on the seat between them, he might clasp it in his again. Much to her surprise and relief, the conversation was easy and continuous over the trip. Kip was the first one in the shed that morning. Removing a harness from a horse had never been so quick or enjoyable.

Ruth was well into her current project, a dainty but sturdy hall seat in oak with Queen Anne feet, before she noticed half the morning was gone. Of course, the morning had gone faster once she'd stopped craning her neck every five minutes to locate Malachi. He'd unconsciously made it easier for her by staying in the office to do some paperwork. As he was there, he attended the shop when the bell heralded the arrival of customers. Ruth hoped they were all legitimate customers and not single women shopping for a husband.

Turning over her sanding block, she ran a finger over the smooth surface. Time to change the paper. She needed to go to a finer grade for this next step anyway. Slipping off her dust mask, Ruth smiled as she recalled her friends' comments about finding it hard to breathe around their beaus. She was beginning to understand what they meant. It had been a rather breathless ride this morning.

She strode over to the cabinet that housed the sheets of sandpaper. Nodding at Gideon, who was changing out the paper on a belt sander, she looked for the grade she needed.

Samuel had been working on a chair leg on the nearby lathe. He shut off the generator-powered machine and rolled his shoulders, understandably stiff after some time in the same position.

"So who are you planning on taking home after the singing next church Sunday, Samuel?" Gideon queried.

Ruth smiled down at the 120-grit sandpaper in her hands. Malachi's younger brothers loved to tease each other. She enjoyed their banter. It made her wish she had siblings.

"It'll be hard to choose. There's so many of them."

Gideon snorted. "How do you know one will go with you?"

"Oh, they will. You just have to know women."

Instead of laughing as she expected, Gideon responded seriously. "Speaking of women, do you think Malachi is missing Leah? He's been acting strange lately."

The grit on the sandpaper roughened Ruth's fingertips as her hands tightened on the sheets. Who was Leah? She'd heard the name mentioned before but hadn't paid much attention. Now the name sounded ominous. In the book of Genesis in the Bible, Leah had sneaked into the wedding ceremony and married Jacob first. He'd eventually gotten Rachel, the one he'd truly wanted, but it had taken him seven more years of working hard for his father-in-law. Ever since reading the story, Ruth had never liked the name of the conniving Leah. She shuffled through a few more grades of sandpaper, her ears focused on the brothers' conversation.

"I don't know. Maybe when she and her father come visit before Christmas, we'll find out."

Ruth stared unseeing at the sandpaper. Her stomach felt like she'd swallowed a woodworking plane outfitted with fresh blades, the knob lodged right under her heart.

"I thought that was all settled before we left Ohio."

"You know Malachi. He never says much about his women."

"*Ja.* Unlike you."

A smile crossed Samuel's handsome face. "There's so much to say about mine. And so many of them to say it about."

With another muffled snort, Gideon settled his safety glasses back on his face and restarted the belt sander. The conversation was over.

So was Ruth's ability to breathe momentarily. Pulling an entirely different grade of sandpaper from the cabinet than the one she'd intended, she slowly made her way to her workstation.

Ruth stared at the Queen Anne legs blankly before remembering what she was working on. Gathering up the pieces, she neatly put that project away. Thoughts whirling, she automatically pulled out the project that gave her comfort. The red oak rocker.

Not wanting to wreck her father's chair, she double-checked the grit on the sandpaper and then began the habitual soothing strokes down the slats that made the surface as smooth as glass. As her hands worked on autopilot, Ruth unfortunately had much time to think. Did Malachi have a girl back in Ohio? She and Hannah had speculated on the possibility. But that was before...he kissed her. Amish courtships were typically kept private until announced at the church a short few weeks before the wedding. Was Malachi betrothed to this Leah?

Ruth sanded vigorously for a moment, but it didn't obliterate the troubling thought. If he was betrothed, why had he kissed her? She vividly recalled her racing heart and the longing to wrap her arms around him.

He didn't seem like the type of man to play with a woman's feelings like that. But what did she know of men really? She hadn't walked out with anyone during her *rumspringa*. And she'd gotten adept at dissuading those who seemed interested, so they stayed just friends.

Daed hadn't remarried after losing his wife, even to help raise a child, in defiance of community expectations. At the thought of her father, Ruth slowed down her mindless stroking and fingered the fine-grained wood. *Oh,* Daed, *I wish you were here for words of advice.* The back of her eyes prickled. Ruth blinked rapidly to prevent the telltale onslaught of tears.

Of course, Leah could be coming here to get ready for the wedding. Traditionally held during the months after harvest until Christmas, Amish weddings were now spread throughout the year. If she was arriving soon, it wasn't too late to get a wedding completed by the year's end.

Would he go back to Ohio, or would she come here to Wisconsin? Surely he wouldn't go back; he'd just bought a home and business. It made sense. He'd come first, get settled in a home and work before a new wife would join him. Setting the wood down, Ruth pressed her fingers to her eyes. It didn't stop the tears from welling up.

That is why you are not going to be an Amish wife, Ruth reminded herself. It would be the loss of hopes and freedoms. Now it was simply the loss of a man. A man she didn't have anyway.

An *Englisch* wife might start her marriage with *I do.* For an Amish wife, a wedding was the beginning of *I don't*s. *I don't get to make furniture. I don't work in the workshop or the store.* Once baptized, which was necessary before one got married, *I don't take a correspondence course.*

She had some more *I don't*s: *I don't want to be here if he's married to someone else. I don't want to see his new wife come in to visit him. I don't want to see her sitting with the married women at church. I don't want to see him growing a beard as a married man, a beard I won't look across and see every morning. I don't want to see her pregnant with his child.*

Her eyes squeezed shut but tears leaked through anyway. Her breath came in shallow pants. *I don't want to see her come in, trailed after by his* kinder. *Boys with solemn blue eyes with just a hint of mischief. Girls with blond hair that'd be curly when long.*

There was sourness in her stomach and the bitter taste of bile at the back of her throat. She was going to be sick. Ruth yanked her safety glasses off and tossed them on the bench. Tears now fell freely. She swiveled on her stool, prepared to make a hasty dash to the bathroom. And found herself facing solemn blue eyes. She couldn't read what was in his eyes at all. She'd never seen them like that. Nor heard the low, flat tone in his voice.

"What are you working on?"

Ruth swallowed hard against the acrid taste in her mouth. If she opened her mouth, she was afraid something other than words would come out.

Malachi raised an eyebrow, his eyes never wavering from hers.

"It's a rocking chair. For me." Ruth managed to get the words out, but just barely. "Something my father started."

His gaze flicked over the pieces of red oak before returning to her face. Ruth wanted to scrub her hands over the mess she knew she presented, but she kept them clenched at her sides. To fret about her looks would've been prideful. She fretted anyway. Pride was conditional on regaining control of herself. Ruth straightened her shoulders and swallowed again.

It was a moment before he spoke. "Shouldn't you be concentrating on something productive for the business during work hours? Since your efforts have made us all so busy?"

Ruth couldn't help it. She gasped. Amish might be nonviolent, but he might as well have punched her. She wished he had—she would've been less hurt. Brushing by him, she beelined for the coatrack and snagged her bonnet and cape from the peg as she swept by. Her shoulder burned from the brief contact. She firmly, but in a controlled manner, shut the door behind her before swinging the cape over her shoulders and fastening her bonnet as she headed briskly down the street.

Malachi watched the black cape swirl briefly in the window of the door before it—and Ruth—disappeared. He felt his sigh down to his brown work shoes. This was why he didn't like to interact with crying females. There was no right move. He couldn't pull her into his arms and comfort her as he longed to do. Absorbing all her cares and sorrows. Not here at work, where his brothers and other employees only had to swivel their heads to watch, if they weren't watching already.

His gaze left the door and swept around the room. Malachi raised an eyebrow at all of them and one by one the men returned to their work. Samuel was the last. He cocked his eyebrow in return, a mocking imitation of his brother. Malachi glared at his sibling. Samuel smirked, dropped his safety glasses down over his eyes and returned his attention to the lathe.

Malachi directed his gaze to the delicately wrought oak pieces at Ruth's station. It was beautiful work. Amos Fisher had been an outstanding master craftsman, and he'd taught his daughter well. But as talented as she was, and as beautiful as he knew the piece would be when finished, Malachi didn't want to see Ruth work on it. It hurt her too much. He saw the pain on her face every time she worked on the rocker.

Remembering the furniture her *daed* had already made her and her melancholy expression when she'd mentioned this unfinished piece, Malachi stroked his finger over the silken wood. That was why he'd interrupted her. She was obviously distraught. He'd wanted to protect her from that pain. Knowing she wouldn't stop if he directly asked her, he'd decided to come at it from a different angle. An angle that supported her value to the business while getting her to stop working on something that upset her.

Malachi glanced at the closed door. Obviously it'd been the wrong angle. Casting one last considering look at the oak, he shook his head. Crying women. Safer to stick your fingers in a malfunctioning table saw. Sighing, he made his way to the office door.

Knowing Ruth brought her lunch, Malachi kept checking the workshop for her return during the lunch break. He stopped looking when Jacob returned from lunch at the café and mentioned he'd run into Hannah

Lapp, who was giving Ruth a ride home as she didn't feel well. Malachi furrowed his brow. She'd been fine this morning. And very fine last night.

After everyone else left for the day and weekend, Malachi wandered into the workshop to Ruth's work area again. Eyeing the red oak pieces scattered across the bench where she'd left them in her hasty departure, he picked up a slat and gently slapped it across his palm.

It was later than usual when he left the shop. Malachi's mind was still on Ruth as he harnessed a lonely Kip in the shed. She might be able to avoid him tonight, and this weekend, but she wouldn't be able to do so on Monday. They were meeting with a customer in Portage that morning, a meeting Ruth had set up herself. Malachi didn't think she'd miss it.

They'd hired an *Englisch* driver to take them on the forty-mile round-trip to the larger town. The driver would pick them up at their homes on Monday morning before chauffeuring them to the furniture store in Portage and then back to work afterward. Beyond hanging out the window of the vehicle, there wasn't much she could do to avoid him on the trip. And perhaps he'd talk with his brothers about borrowing one of their rigs to take her home after work Monday. Bess would still be out of commission, leaving Ruth to make her way on foot. Maybe he'd commandeer Gideon's rig this time.

Malachi smiled grimly. Even with the wild ride, or perhaps because of it, Samuel's filly had done him a favor. Maybe he ought to give her another chance. Malachi shook his head, listening to the steady clop of

Kip's hooves on the blacktop. He hadn't had so many complicated females to handle back in Ohio. Only a very subdued but straightforward one. Clicking to Kip to pick up his speed, Malachi determined he liked the twists and turns of the Wisconsin landscape better.

Chapter Fourteen

On Saturday, Ruth dusted every piece of furniture in the house, lingering over the items made by her father. She swept and scrubbed the floors, cleaned the bathroom, even tackled a closet and cleaned out the fireplace. An Amish proverb advised that women's work wasn't seen unless it wasn't done. Hers hadn't been done in a while. And she needed something to occupy her mind and her time.

Her cheeks flushed in remembrance of her actions yesterday. They'd been out of character. She wasn't an evader. Besides, none of that might even come to pass. She was always thinking of what-ifs in terms of the business. There'd never been a man in her life to think about. With Malachi, she'd gotten carried away.

Always pragmatic about business opportunities, she'd be pragmatic about this, as well. Malachi had never mentioned Leah. His brothers didn't know everything. As much as Samuel might think he knew women, well, he didn't. Ruth wrinkled her nose. Not that she was an expert. All women didn't think like her. Particularly those in the Amish community.

Monday she'd see Malachi. She'd ask him. They'd straighten things out. His kisses had to have meant something, right? They'd meant something to her.

That Sunday, one without church, Ruth spent time working on her accounting correspondence course. She didn't consider it work, as she enjoyed the challenge. It was what she'd always dreamed of. Today, she wasn't finding it as fulfilling as she'd anticipated. While staring at the words and numbers, she'd catch herself thinking of other things. Things like the cushiony rustle of straw under her back while blue eyes looked into hers. Or cool fingers brushing across her cheek.

By the time she finished the first assignment, she'd worn down half an eraser. Rubbing it again across the paper, she hoped the score on this assignment wouldn't permanently ruin her grade for the course.

When Rascal uttered his version of a warning bark and scrambled over to the kitchen door, Ruth was happy for the interruption. Sundays without church were used in the Amish community to visit friends and relatives. During her father's illness, Ruth had gotten out of the habit. Just getting through the workweek had tired him out. They'd stayed home on weekends so he could rest.

They had no close family in the area, as both sets of grandparents had passed away while Ruth was growing up. Although he'd been a business owner, Amos had been a private person. As Ruth grew older, she'd taken on more of the business aspects and interaction with people that were essential to the operation, and he'd stayed in the workshop. Yes, they'd been a part of the fabric of the community, hosting church services when it was their turn, supporting others in need, but they'd mostly been on the periphery. A quilt block lining the edge of the blanket as opposed to one in the center of the quilt.

After her father had died, Ruth had been so busy managing the business day to day, and then preparing it for sale that Visiting Sundays had continued to be ones of rest. Or more accurately, of seclusion. Perhaps that'd been a mistake. Perhaps it was time to become a more active part of the community. Then again— Ruth glanced at the paperwork spread over the table as she rose to her feet—it wouldn't matter if she wasn't staying.

A genuine smile lit her face when she opened the door as far as the bouncing pup would let her. *"Guder Nammidaag!"*

Hannah was standing on the porch, a corresponding smile on her pretty face.

"Good afternoon to you, too." Hannah knelt to rub Rascal's ears when the pup dashed outside to place his paw on her black-enclosed legs. "And good afternoon to you, as well. Have you been behaving?"

"There's a reason his name is Rascal." Ruth motioned her in and closed the door behind them. "I suppose all his siblings are perfectly behaved puppies."

"If they are, they're behaving in someone else's homes."

Ruth hurriedly piled her studies into a stack on the table and invited Hannah to sit down. Hannah glanced at the paperwork but didn't say anything as she took a seat. Ruth went to the stove to get them some coffee. "You've sold them all, then?"

"*Ja*. They were gone as soon as they could be weaned."

"I'm not surprised. You have a reputation for raising *wunderbar* puppies." Hannah changed the subject, to Ruth's dismay. "I wanted to see how you were. You seemed quite upset on Friday."

Ruth focused on the cups she was assembling for coffee. "I wanted to thank you for the ride home. And for not asking questions, when I looked pretty…questionable." She'd looked like something that had been dragged face-first after a plow. At least that was how she'd felt.

"I'm asking now." Hannah's voice was gentle. But intractable. When Ruth didn't speak, Hannah did. "Was it something to do with Malachi?"

Bringing the cups to the table, Ruth cringed. "Does everyone know?"

"No, because everyone doesn't know you. Well?"

Ruth sat down across from her friend. "I don't know. Sometimes, when I'm with him, I think…" Ruth paused and flipped her hand in a few small circles. It was hard to put into words what she thought. She glanced at the paperwork stacked on the end of the table. "Then other times, I'm unsure."

Hannah nodded, a sweet smile of understanding on her lovely face. Ruth studied her friend as Hannah lifted the coffee cup. Whereas Ruth questioned her place in the Amish community, Hannah was the epitome of a perfect young Amish woman. Filled with patience, *demut* and *gelassenheit*. The Amish discouraged photos, but if there were ever a poster of the essence of an Amish woman, it would have Hannah's picture on it. In the current state of Ruth's muddled mind, she didn't know how one could sincerely display such submission, or "letting be." A glaring omission in her own character that Ruth needed to pray about tonight. Again.

She didn't tell Hannah she was planning on leaving the Amish. Her friend wouldn't understand.

Hannah set the cup down. "Since you're going to share so much on that, I'll tell you the other purpose of my visit. I'm inviting you to the cookie exchange we're having at my family's home before Christmas. *Ach*, I can read it in your face. Don't say no." Reaching across the table, Hannah set her hand on Ruth's. "It's been too long since you've joined in any of these activities." She smiled gently. "I know you've been terribly busy for a long time, but we'd like you to come."

When Ruth didn't respond, Hannah continued, "Your quilting skills might be rather dismal for the bees, but I know you've a few cookie recipes that are edible."

Ruth squeezed Hannah's hand before she let it go and stood up. As she'd thought earlier, perhaps it was time to join in more often. Whether she stayed or left the community, it would be *gut* for her. "Since you asked so charmingly, how could I refuse?"

Hannah laughed as she also stood. "I'll get you the details later." She leaned over and patted Rascal's head before she walked to the door. "In the meantime, I hope things go well for you at work." With a meaningful smile, she left.

On Monday, by the time a blue car drove up the lane, Ruth had been ready for over two hours. After giving Rascal some extra attention, she'd focused on her coursework. As the vehicle rolled to a halt, Ruth stood with a barking Rascal by her side, looking beyond it to the red flag sticking up over the mailbox containing her completed assignment. Tying her bonnet under her chin, she stepped out on the porch. She greeted the *Englisch* driver with a brief smile.

Waving to the driver, Mr. Thompson, to stay in his seat when he started to get out and open the door for her, Ruth opened the rear door, got in and sat down. Closing the door with a thunk, she was very conscious of Malachi's presence on the opposite side of the seat. She tucked her cape underneath her and crossed her ankles, trying to take up as little space as possible.

"Good morning," Mr. Thompson greeted cheerfully. "I hope you don't mind, I invited my wife along for the trip. She had some shopping she wanted to do in Portage. We thought we could do that while you conduct your business."

"That's fine," Ruth assured him. Mr. Thompson had driven her and her *daed* many times and she'd met his wife before. He was dependable and friendly. He was also chatty. And she wasn't feeling too chatty this morning. "You two go ahead and visit. I've got some things I want to think about."

Mr. and Mrs. Thompson seemed content with that and started a constant hum of conversation in the front seat. What, or actually who, Ruth wanted to think about, was eyeing her closely. She flashed him what she hoped would pass for a smile and focused her attention on the snow-covered landscape outside her window. If her hand drifted from her lap to lie palm down on the seat between them, and his strong calloused one slid from his lap to rest with only a short inch separating their little fingers, it was enough. For now.

Henry Morrow greeted them with a smile when the chime heralded their arrival into the Portage Emporium a while later. Hastening over, he shook their hands and took their outer garments. "I'm so glad to meet you in person. Business by phone used to seem impersonal. When it's by fax, it gets even more so." His eyes rounded, in almost-comical shock, as if he'd just realized that what he said might sound offensive.

Ruth smiled, feeling like it was her first genuine smile of the day. She'd been through this before with the *Englisch*. They wanted Amish-crafted furniture but weren't so thrilled about dealing with Amish practices. "Don't worry. It's nothing we haven't heard before. We appreciate you working with us on what is required by our *Ordnung*." The Miller's Creek *Ordnung*, the set of rules that district members lived by, didn't allow phones to be owned by its members.

Malachi removed his black felt hat and handed it over. "In fact, Ruth has worked out a relationship with the local café where they can take phone messages for us, in case you need to communicate with more urgency than fax."

Ruth shot a glance at Malachi and raised her eyebrow at the encouraging smile. They'd had a rather heated discussion on the topic last week. Ruth had come up with the idea of offering the Dew Drop Inn one small piece of discounted furniture a month in exchange for the use of their phone and message receptions. The café could feature the item for its Amish and increasing *Englisch* customers, selling it at a profit that would cover the inconvenience of the use. The discreet tag on the piece of furniture would direct potential customers to the shop. The owner of the café had accepted the proposal with eagerness. Malachi had taken a little more convincing.

"Wonderful!" Mr. Morrow responded enthusiastically as Ruth gave him the number of the café. "We've had such interest in your furniture since we added it to our collection. Folks have asked about pieces in different stains and lead times on special orders. Being able to get information while they're still in the store would be extremely helpful. Strike while the iron is hot, you know."

He and Malachi fell into a discussion of lead times, as well as wood and stain options as Mr. Morrow led them to his office. They passed an open door. Ruth peeked inside to see a young woman doing paperwork at a desk. Returning the woman's easy smile, Ruth sucked in a breath as she took in the rest of the room. It was larger than most offices. Large enough to comfortably accommodate the child who sprawled on the carpet, busy coloring in a book, and the playpen against the wall. Ruth could see the hump of a miniature figure under a blanket and the tiny hand of the *bobbeli* that slept there. She blinked at the surprising pressure at the back of her eyes. Nodding at the woman, Ruth hurried on.

Her heartbeat picked up its pace as she followed the sound of the men's voices. This was what she wanted. All. She wanted it all. She yearned for a husband and children but she wanted more. She wanted to learn. She wanted to continue working at something more than the summer produce stands or quilt making, which were some of the only things Amish women in their district were allowed to do after they were married. To get all she wanted—the office with children a few paces back down the hall—she couldn't have an Amish husband.

She couldn't have…him. Ruth caught up to the voices. Malachi was in Mr. Morrow's doorway, his broad shoulder propped against the doorjamb. His thick blond hair showed the indentation of his missing hat, the ends threatening to curl below the crease. His lean cheek dimpled above a smile at something the store owner must have said. He turned at Ruth's approach and she sucked in another breath at the look in his blue eyes. A look that seemed to say, "I've been waiting for you. Here you are."

Ruth drifted to a halt, her heart thumping. She'd been waiting for him, as well. If she could have him, all the other things didn't matter. She had to cross her arms over her chest to stop herself from reaching for him.

Malachi furrowed his brow at Ruth. She had a funny look on her face. He was glad they seemed to be beyond whatever had been going on last Friday. All weekend she'd been on his mind, to the point where he'd almost driven over to see her. So he'd kept himself busy. Samuel had tested his nonviolent tendencies by smirking at him every time Malachi looked up. Only Mr. Thompson's occasional glance in the rearview mirror this morning had stifled the urge to clasp her hand during the trip. He wouldn't leave Ruth open to gossip.

She seemed stuck in the hallway. Malachi motioned her toward the office door. "Mr. Morrow has some questions that you could answer better than I." He stepped aside to have her enter the office and take the seat the store owner indicated. Malachi settled into the one beside it.

"We can't keep your product in the store. It sells out as fast as we can stock it. All the dining room sets were gone in the pre-Thanksgiving rush."

"That was all Ruth's doing. I was just getting into the picture then."

"Well, let me tell you, she does a fantastic job. Both as a craftswoman and as a business manager."

Ruth folded her hands in her lap. "Thanks. I've been taking correspondence courses to learn as much as possible."

Malachi raised his eyebrow. She had? That was news to him. Amish women normally didn't have formal education beyond eighth grade. And none after they were baptized.

"Well, it shows," Mr. Morrow agreed heartily. "I've been bragging on you, little lady. You ever want to move to Portage, or even Madison, folks would be lined up to hire you."

Ruth smiled demurely. Malachi's eyebrows took a dip, not knowing which he liked less in the comments. *Bragging* certainly wasn't a word used frequently in the Amish community. In fact, humility was a tenet of their faith. And he definitely didn't like the thought of anyone else, particularly in communities distant to Miller's Creek, hiring Ruth. His fingers curled around the wooden armrests of the chair. Time to hurry this conversation along.

Much like Sour Grapes, Samuel's spoiled filly, Malachi took the bit in his teeth in terms of the appointment. Further business discussions were quickly concluded. A short time and an expanded arrangement later, he and Ruth stood. Malachi touched the slender small of her back to guide her out of the office before he could catch himself. Fingers tingling from the contact, he pulled his hand back.

Waving their goodbyes after a quick tour of the operation, they stepped out onto the sidewalk to find Mr. Thompson's blue car parked along the street a short distance away.

Ruth looked at him with a smile. *"Gut?"*

If his hand brushed hers as they walked down the surprisingly busy sidewalk, it was an accident. At least that was what Malachi told himself. "Very *gut*."

"I'm glad. Increased business helps provide employment. You might have to expand."

Malachi's smile was a little brittle—his mind was still focused on the store owner's comment about opportunities for Ruth. "I think we can at least keep everyone employed."

After exchanging greetings with the waiting *Englisch* couple in the car and declining their question regarding an early lunch, they started on the ride home.

The Thompsons seemed to find a lot to talk about in the front seat. In contrast, Ruth was unnaturally quiet. But her hand lay palm up on the seat between them. Malachi extended his so his little finger bumped hers when the car bounced over some railroad tracks.

They'd just passed the sign for the city limits when Ruth spoke quietly. "Who's Leah?"

Malachi went still at the question. Eyes guarded, he swiveled his head to look into wary green ones.

He lowered his brows. "Where'd you hear that name?" If his tone was harsher than normal, well, for sure and certain, he didn't want to discuss Leah with Ruth.

"Your *brieder* mentioned her."

Malachi frowned. If his brothers made any unfavorable comparison of the two women within Ruth's hearing, he'd take them out behind the barn and be more brother than Amish. The two women were nothing alike. Which was why his feelings for Ruth were much different than any he'd had about Leah.

"Her father owned the furniture business I supervised in Ohio." That'd been the extent of the relationship. Even though Leah and her father had given enough hints that they'd be agreeable to a much closer one.

"So you know her well." Her slender shoulders slumped a little. Malachi wasn't sure if that was the reason her hand shifted closer to the black cape. He just knew it moved farther away from his hand and out of touching distance.

Malachi thought of Leah. She'd worked in the store part of the business but always seemed to be back in the workshop, underfoot. No, *underfoot* wasn't the right word. Leah had more finesse than that. But around. Available. Sweet. Undemanding. Agreeable. All the things the woman beside him wasn't. His lips quirked. Yes, very unlike his badger.

"*Ja.* I know her very well." Ruth shot him a glance,

her eyes pausing briefly on the smile before she faced the back of Mr. Thompson's head.

"She is coming here before Christmas?"

"Ja." He said nothing more. There was nothing more to say. Leah and her father were coming to visit his aunt. The Solomon King and Moses Lapp families had been close prior to Aunt Miriam's move to Wisconsin years ago. It was highly likely he'd see them while they were in the area, as his aunt would surely invite his brothers and him over for supper some evening.

If Leah and Solomon were coming to Wisconsin for a different agenda, they were heading for disappointment. They weren't his guests. Malachi pressed his lips together. There was nothing more to say.

Apparently, there was nothing more for Ruth to say, either. She was quiet the rest of the journey home, her hands now clasped in her lap. Malachi surreptitiously flicked his eyes in her direction several times during the remainder of the journey, hoping her hand would rest on the seat between them so he could curl his own around it.

It never did.

Chapter Fifteen

On Tuesday, Ruth walked down to Hannah's farm and caught a ride into town with her. She'd informed Malachi of her plans Monday afternoon when they'd returned to the workshop after the trip to Portage. He hadn't said anything in response, just regarded her with solemn eyes until Ruth had to bite her tongue not to squirm.

Tuesday morning started out well. Malachi had apparently found much to do in the office and stayed out of the workshop, which was a relief for Ruth. It wasn't until later in the day she discovered there might be other things keeping him out front.

The petite rolltop desk was finished. Prior to preparing an item for shipping, it was their custom to place a discreet business card in a drawer. Ruth searched where the cards were generally stored in the workshop but didn't find any. She frowned as she walked toward the office. They needed to order more anyway. The previous ones had stated Fisher Furniture. New ones that read Schrock Brothers Furniture needed to be made.

Particularly now that there wouldn't be a Fisher involved in the business much longer.

Ruth paused for a moment in front of the door. She ached a little every time she saw him. *Ach*, she ached when she didn't see him as well, but she'd work on that. And he wouldn't be witnessing his impact on her anyway. When she knew she was going to see him, she would be in control. Prepared.

Inhaling deeply, she briskly pushed the door open. Nothing could prepare her for what she saw as she stepped through. Malachi was not in the office, as she'd expected, but was in the store. With his hand clasped around the delicate one of a beautiful stranger. Ruth halted abruptly, her hand on the knob of the still-open door.

The two turned as the sounds of the workshop intruded into the store area. Ruth noted Malachi hastily dropped the woman's hand. She stepped the rest of the way into the store and turned to close the door behind her, squeezing her eyes shut as she placed one hand on the jamb and the other on the knob, pulling it secure. For a moment, it was the only secure thing holding her up.

After exhaling the breath that'd caught in her throat when she'd entered the room, Ruth turned back around. Lack of oxygen made her light-headed, not the sight of Malachi touching another woman. She nodded at the couple and stepped toward the office.

"Excuse me. I just needed to get some business cards for the back. Mr. Schrock, if you haven't yet, you might need to order some new ones with your business name on them." Ruth didn't care if they didn't hear a word she said. She darted through the office door. Jerking open a file drawer, she quickly flipped through the folders. As she'd thought, no cards, old or new. The file was as empty as her heart.

"Ruth." Malachi stood in the office doorway. Ruth stayed bent over the filing cabinet drawer, her back to him. "I'd like you to meet Leah King."

Her eyes squeezed shut. *What if I don't want to meet her?* She straightened, swallowing the bile that sprinkled the back of her throat, and turned to face his watchful eyes. Exiting the office, she bumped into the doorjamb in her effort to avoid touching him as she passed.

The Amish didn't believe in using the words *pretty* or *beautiful* to describe one another. To do so might make one *hochmut*—"proud" or "arrogant." Something definitely not of their Plain world. That didn't mean they didn't know what beautiful was. Or how attractive it was to the opposite sex. During her *rumspringa*, Ruth had purchased plenty of *Englisch* magazines. There'd been pictures of beautiful women in them.

Even without makeup, the woman before her could hold her own with the *Englisch* models.

Leah looked like a perfectly put together quilt. No stitch was out of place. The materials chosen were impeccable—the gold of the hair, the violet of the eyes, the pink of the cheeks. The design was flawless. Ruth looked like a quilt she might make, mismatched materials and sloppy stitching. She remembered the sawdust on her neck, gently blown off by Malachi. Now, instead of the memory making her smile, she wanted to cry. She was likely covered with the dust of the trade again.

Ruth curled stain-shadowed fingers into her palms. She might work with him, but before her was what a man wanted to go home to.

Leah even had a lovely, serene smile for Ruth. One Ruth couldn't return. Had this been Jacob's Leah from the book of Genesis, he would've stopped after marrying her and forgone the other seven years of working for Rachel. Who needed a Rachel when you had this Leah?

If Malachi had introduced Ruth to Leah as well, Ruth didn't hear it over the buzzing in her ears. She gave a curt nod at the vision that had been holding Malachi's hand, and headed into the workshop, to a world where she belonged. Or at least, one in which she used to belong, she thought as she stiffly strode back to her workstation, clenching her tongue between her teeth to keep any expression from showing on her face.

Reaching her station, she stared unseeing at the empty workbench. What had she been doing? Oh, yes, she was preparing the desk for shipment. Ruth clasped and unclasped her hands, trying to relax. She'd been looking for a card to place in the drawer. She'd have to ask Malachi what he wanted to do since the cards weren't available. Later. She'd ask later. She certainly wasn't going back in there now.

And now was not a good time to start on another project. She'd either waste the wood, injure herself—she winced at the memory of another injury and the moments of closeness afterward—or she'd disappoint a customer with shoddy workmanship. A glance at the wall clock determined it was close to lunchtime. Interest in food was far from her mind, but escaping briefly was very tempting.

Ruth swallowed. Thankfully, her stomach acted like it was going to stay in place but she didn't want to put anything in it right now. But if she couldn't escape physically, she'd escape mentally. Even if it were into a piece that Malachi didn't approve of her working on during his time. Ruth's lips firmed. Maybe now would be the best time to work on something he didn't approve of. Besides, working on the chair made Ruth feel close to *Daed*. Although it was painful, too, she needed that sensation now, when her heart and mind were racing and she felt on the edge of a precipice.

She turned to where she kept the red oak pieces. They weren't there. Ruth searched under the workbench and in the areas where she kept other projects. No red oak. Quickly rounding the end of her workbench, she checked workstations nearby. Still nothing. Her actions drew questioning looks from others in the workshop.

Numbly walking back to her workstation, Ruth concentrated on the last time she'd seen the chair. She went still as the memory surfaced. Friday. When she'd just learned of Leah. When Malachi had chastised her for working on it. She'd stormed out and left it. And it was now gone.

The door to the store opened and Malachi stepped through, immediately looking to her. Ruth met his gaze and didn't blink as he walked through the shop.

"Where's my *daed*'s rocker?" Ruth didn't recognize her voice when he was close enough for her to ask without shouting the question that burned through her. She did recognize the subsequent guilt she read in his face.

"You took it," she said bleakly.

He pressed his lips together but made no response.

Ruth turned away. Any energy she'd possessed swept out of her and she just felt…empty. "Just go. Please, go," she whispered to the nicked bench that filled her vision.

When she looked over a moment later, he was gone. Placing her hands on the counter, she dropped her head between her shoulders. A tear escaped from her eye, rolled down her nose and splattered on the wooden surface. How long ago was it that she'd been in this very spot, missing her *daed*, concerned the new owner would take away her chance to work with the wood, something she loved?

How ironic that here she was again, crying. Willing to give up woodworking if only she could have the new owner for her own.

Malachi walked back through the workshop. He could have sawed off all his fingers and he wouldn't have noticed. All he could feel was the pain evident in Ruth's eyes. He had no words against that kind of heartache. Maybe what he'd done was wrong, but it'd been done for her.

All morning he'd been trying to think of something to say that would breach whatever happened between them on the ride home yesterday. Something about Leah's pending visit had disturbed her. Before he could think of a way to broach the subject, the bell had jangled as the store door opened and Leah had come in. Malachi hadn't been expecting their visit this early. Correction—he hadn't been expecting their part of the visit to him this early.

He'd shaken her hand, asking after her and Solomon's well-being, when Ruth stepped through the shop door, a stunned look on her face. She'd slipped quickly into the office. Not knowing what else to do in the situation, he'd introduced the two women. From what he'd glimpsed of Ruth's face as she dashed back out the door, that'd been a mistake.

Turning to follow her, not sure what he'd do beyond wrapping his arms around her when he caught her, Malachi had felt a gentle touch on his sleeve.

"Your aunt and I came into town to do a little shopping. Miriam was drawn into a discussion at the quilt shop." Leah smiled charmingly. "I wanted to see your store. We thought you might give me a ride to the bishop's home, where my *daed* is visiting as she didn't know how long she'd be."

Malachi looked at her blankly, thinking that she'd be able to walk to the place faster than he could harness his horse and drive her there. He shot a glance at the closed workroom door. Perhaps he could ask Samuel to give Leah the ride, while he checked on Ruth. Samuel never minded driving with a pretty girl.

Good manners and appreciation for the opportunities Leah's father had given him over the years made him reluctantly nod. But, he resolved, good manners wouldn't prevent him from making himself scarce during the rest of their visit to his aunt. Good manners also didn't stop him from telling Leah to wait in the store while he checked something in the shop. Ruth.

Never, in all his years of working with furniture, had trying to make something better actually made it worse. Returning to the store after seeing Ruth—seeing her devastated for some reason she wouldn't say—Malachi noticed his hand trembling as it closed around the knob.

He paused and exhaled slowly. After stepping through the door, he closed it on the normally comforting sounds of the shop and turned to see Leah watching him, a smile on her beautiful face.

"Are you ready?"

Malachi's eyes swept over her. There wasn't anything out of place. Except her presence in his business and life.

"*Ja.*"

If Kip was surprised about the unexpected outing in the middle of the day, Malachi wasn't. It seemed to be Leah's way. She never outright asked. She sweetly maneuvered. With quiet, gentle nudges.

Malachi didn't like it. But he'd always allowed himself to be nudged along.

It was a primary reason he'd left Ohio. He was afraid he'd be nudged right into standing in front of the district as the bishop joined them as man and wife. It was obviously what Leah and her father wanted. As to what Malachi wanted, well, it hadn't felt right. It'd felt like a harness collar that didn't fit well. After a while the collar would wear a hole in his hide. And who knew how long the nudging would stay gentle.

Malachi took his time harnessing the gelding. It was some time later when he poked his head in the store door and advised Leah the buggy was out front. If she'd wanted to check out the shop, she'd had plenty of time. Hopefully enough so she wouldn't need to come back.

Climbing up by the wheel, he felt somewhat churlish when he didn't offer Leah assistance into the buggy. She gave him a sweet smile, but her eyes reflected surprise as she settled into the seat on his left side. A wife's side, Malachi noted sourly as he gathered the reins. Leah gracefully tucked her cape around her and Malachi signaled Kip to head out.

Malachi glanced over at the perfect profile visible just beyond the edge of her black bonnet. Returning his attention to the horse in front of him, he sighed. Yes, she was perfect, but for someone else. Not him. He clicked to Kip, who picked up his pace. Malachi's tense shoulders began to relax. The sooner he delivered Leah to her father, the better.

Kip made Malachi think of his new Belgian geldings. And another way to encourage plodding companions other than nudging. Jeb, the older Belgian, would get the field plowed or the lumber hauled in a slow and steady pace. It was his teaming with eager and enthusiastic Huck that got work done more quickly, and Malachi could tell, more enjoyably, for the pair. Malachi's lips quirked. Kind of like him. And…his badger. He could put his shoulders into the collar every day and pull willingly to accomplish things, but it was being in harness with Ruth that brought joy and passion to those accomplishments.

Malachi sat up straighter at the realization. Leah looked over and smiled. Sweetly. Gently. Her right hand gracefully dropped, palm up, to the seat between them. Malachi kept his focus on the straps of leather and brown back that moved in steady rhythm ahead of him. He could still see the hand rested on the seat. Kip's ears flicked back at the instructions that telegraphed down the reins to move faster. Malachi subtly shifted to the right until his elbow brushed the side of the buggy.

* * *

"Everything all right?"

Ruth wasn't surprised at Rebecca's question. She forced her stiff lips to smile and strove to ignore what she knew were red-rimmed eyes.

"Everything's fine, thanks," she lied to the waitress, trying not to wince as she said the words. Everything was far from fine. Which was why she was taking action. *Do not ask the Lord to guide your footsteps if you are not willing to move your feet.* The proverb popped into her head. *I'm moving my feet, Lord. I just omitted the asking part.*

A grimace edged across Ruth's face. She had no excuse not to ask *Gott* to guide her steps. It was why she always wore the *kapp*. Women covered their heads when they prayed. As they were to pray continually, the *kapp* was always worn.

But if it was *Gott*'s will that she stay, why would He make it so painful? So it must be His will that she go. And it was what she wanted, so she was keeping her promise to *Daed* that she choose her path. She was simply going to move her feet before she could change her mind.

"I just need to use the phone."

"Oh, sure," the young woman agreed before turning to the next customer with a smile. A big smile. Even in her misery, Ruth turned her head to see who was greeted with such enthusiasm, then instantly wished she hadn't. It was Samuel. Of course.

She whipped around and hunched her shoulders, trying to make herself smaller or, hopefully, even disappear before he saw her. It didn't work. She caught his quizzical glance at her before he flashed a smile that matched the one the pretty waitress offered him. Ruth waited for a minute before she picked up the phone receiver, hoping Rebecca would ring him up and he'd move on. No such luck. Samuel was in full flirt mode and Rebecca was a willing recipient. She even rang up a few other customers, who looked askance at Ruth as they passed her hovering at the end of the counter.

Sighing, Ruth lifted the receiver and dialed the number she'd memorized. As she listened to it ring, she cleared her throat several times. Maybe no one would pick up and she wouldn't have to do this. No. It had to be done. She drummed her fingers on the countertop to drown out the sound of the man's voice behind her. The voice that was too much like his brother's.

"Hello, Mr. Morrow? This is Ruth Fisher of Fisher Furn—I mean Schrock Brothers Furniture. Yes. I'm fine, thank you. How are you doing? That's *gut* to hear." She let the man ramble on for a moment. He talked even faster than she did.

"Say, Mr. Morrow," Ruth interjected when he took a breath. She hunched around the phone, dropping the volume of her voice. "When we visited you earlier, you mentioned you knew of a few people in Portage or Madison who might be interested in hiring me if I was available. I was wondering if you could provide some names and numbers."

Ruth squeezed her eyes shut as Mr. Morrow exclaimed over this request. Although not listening, she was throbbingly conscious of the conversation behind her and who was in it. "Yes, yes. I realize it's a big step. But it's one I'm ready to make. Things have changed here and I…I need to make a change, as well." A tear dripped down from her compressed eyes and splashed on the black plastic phone. Opening her eyes, Ruth hastily wiped it off.

"If you could give me a few names now, that'd be wonderful. Yes, you know we're not available at phones for a callback. Yes, I'll wait." Briefly and painfully. Her heart thumped with every second as Mr. Morrow apparently pulled up a computer screen. "Yes, I'm ready. Okay, got that. And the next? Could you please repeat those last two numbers?" She struggled to make the pen mark on the sweat-dampened note in her hand. "Okay. No, that's enough for now. Thanks so much, Mr. Morrow."

Carefully setting the receiver into the cradle, Ruth muttered thanks to a distracted Rebecca and hustled out the café door. Once outside, she flicked a quick glance back through the glass windows that fronted the café. To her relief, Samuel wasn't paying any attention to her. And as she had his attention, Rebecca wasn't, either.

Pent-up energy ebbed out of Ruth. She managed to get two storefronts down before she leaned against a hitching post, knees weak from making the call and the realization of the change in her life that she'd just implemented. She blew out a deep breath. Perhaps it was possible to go back.

The rapid tattoo of hoofbeats filtered through her bonnet. Turning her head, she saw a bay coming down the street. It was Kip. In the buggy was Malachi, his face turned in conversation to Leah, seated on his left. Where Leah would continue to sit with Malachi.

Ruth watched them travel down the street and turn the corner.

No. Going back wasn't possible.

Malachi looked up from the onerous task of accounting to see Samuel prop a broad shoulder against the door frame. He frowned. Samuel never sought him out in the office. If he had something to talk about, he'd call Malachi over when he was in the workshop or wait to discuss it at home over chores or supper.

"Well, big *bruder.* I don't know what you did, but apparently you did it with your standard flair for effectiveness."

Setting his pencil down, Malachi swiveled the wooden desk chair to meet his brother full on. Something in Samuel's normally irreverent tone conveyed that complete attention was necessary. Attention that'd been fractured since Ruth had stared at him with devastated eyes.

Since returning from driving Leah to meet her father at the bishop's house, he'd thought of nothing but Ruth, which was why he'd pulled the accounting out to punish himself. Several times he'd sprung from the desk chair to pace to the workshop door, only to return and plop down in the chair again. He didn't know yet what to say to settle whatever was going on in that active mind of hers.

She was a reasonable woman. Normally. Sometimes. Maybe his drive home would provide time to consider a reasonable response. He'd leave a little early and stop by the shop where Hannah worked and let her know he'd be picking up Ruth in the morning. It was unlikely

Ruth would jump out once she was in the buggy, regardless of what she thought of their conversation. It'd be a good time to talk. Maybe she'd calm down overnight, a little at least. If people started speculating from the frequent buggy rides that they were walking out— Malachi shuffled that around in his mind much as a horse might work a new bit in his mouth—maybe that wasn't a bad thing.

"She's leaving."

Malachi was confused with Samuel's flat statement. "Of course she is. She and her *daed* weren't planning to stay long."

"I don't mean Leah. I mean the other one. The one you want, big *bruder*. Ruth is leaving."

"What?" Malachi stood up so fast the wooden desk chair rocked against his leg. Its motion slowed much faster than his suddenly racing heart.

"Just overheard her using the phone at the Dew Drop. She called a Mr. Morrow." Samuel's eyes quirked toward Malachi to see if the name meant anything to his brother. Reading that it did, he continued, "She was asking about names and numbers of people in Portage and Madison that might want to hire her. She said something about needing to make a change. I think you had a change in mind for her, as well. But I don't believe it was this one."

When Malachi's gaze darted to the workshop door, Samuel straightened from his slouch against the doorjamb. "She's not there. You've got some work to do, *bruder*." He shook his head. "When I find the woman I might want to marry, I'm going to make it a lot less complicated than you."

Staring at the door, Malachi eased back into his chair. He didn't like complicated, either. How did it get to this point? How did he fix it? As he gazed unseeingly out the office window to the well-ordered showroom beyond, things finally started to fall into place like the handcrafted furniture it displayed. Intricately, seamlessly, beautifully.

He wanted Ruth for his wife. It was as simple as that. He'd come to Miller's Creek for a business and had found a match. Now if only he could make Ruth see that, as well.

Chapter Sixteen

Bits of red rubber flew across the lamp-lit table as Ruth furiously erased what she'd just written. She slumped back in her chair and tossed the now-eraserless pencil onto the table. If she hadn't already gone back and forth several times between knitting and the coursework tonight, she'd go back to knitting again. But she'd dropped two stitches on one row of the much-abused afghan and picked up three stitches the following row. Those were just the mistakes she was aware of. It was a mess. So was Ruth.

The pup lay at her feet under the table. Even he was tired of the pacing back and forth. Ruth curled her toes to keep her foot from tapping and stayed put, although her eyes returned to the mound of yarn in the rocker. She sucked in and blew out a breath in a long huff.

Usually her knitting, unlike her inept quilting, was impeccable. And calming. Nothing was calming tonight. Ruth's mind churned as much as her stomach. The challenge with the knitting wasn't just this evening. She'd been making one mistake after another on the project. Several rows required ripping out and re-doing, an exercise Ruth despised.

She frowned at the pile of dark blue. The pup raised his head at a few escaped foot taps. How far down did it need to be ripped out? The rows had been neat and organized. Until she met Malachi. No, she'd managed to keep it together beyond that. The stitching had gotten uneven when she'd fallen in love with him.

Crossing her arms on the paperwork strewed over the kitchen table, Ruth dropped her head upon them. *Experience is a hard teacher*, the old adage said. *She gives the test first and the lesson afterward.* Ruth clenched her jaw. She'd failed the test. Miserably. She'd done the opposite of what she'd planned—she'd fallen in love with an Amish man.

Ruth bit her lower lip as another unwanted homily surfaced. *Advice when most needed is least heeded.* She hadn't listened to her own advice. If she had, she wouldn't have fallen in love. And definitely not with a man who already had a sweetheart. How foolish was that?

I will not cry, she vowed as she pushed off the table, though her lips felt numb and her eyes hurt. Sitting back, she stared at the papers spread over the table's surface. The writing on the pages could be hieroglyphics for all she saw.

Apparently it was *Gott*'s will for her to leave Miller's Creek. Because she certainly couldn't stay. Not now. An Amish man had tempted her from her path. Ruth pressed her lips together to prevent a sob. But *Gott* had wisely put an obstacle in that direction. Malachi's already-chosen match. So Ruth's path must lie in another direction. One she'd finally set in motion.

Her eyes wandered around the home she'd grown up in. The one she'd shared with her *daed*. She looked at the furniture pieces he'd made. Those would go with her, of course. Even if she had to cram them into a tiny apartment with considerably less space than the rambling farmhouse had. But all her memories of her father were here or at the shop or somewhere in the community. And he wouldn't be around to make new ones in new places with her anymore.

A few shallow breaths fought off her threatening nausea. She calmed herself with the realization that she didn't have to sell the farm. The acreage could be rented, while the house remained available for her to stay in. Should she come back for a visit. Or return permanently, if the *Englisch* world wasn't all she hoped it to be.

But if she stayed in the Amish community, she'd already disregarded the other husband prospects here. She'd be an old maid. Bile crept up the back of Ruth's throat. The pain of that stigma and loneliness would be less than the ache of seeing a married Malachi every day and every other Sunday at church. Assuming she could get her job back.

Dropping her chin, she tried to focus on the rows of numbers in front of her. *Concentrate on this. This test you won't fail.* With a sigh, Ruth shoved the coursework to one side of the table. The challenge of learning didn't bring the joy it once did. The pencil rolled and dropped to the floor with a clatter, and the puppy scrambled after it.

Ruth wearily got up, amazed at how tired just trying not to cry made her, and picked up the pencil before Rascal gnawed on it with his needle-sharp teeth. Picking him up as well, she rested her chin on his head.

"Let's go to bed. I can't seem to do much else."

Rascal sensed her mood and did his business without his standard exploration when they went for their nightly trek outside.

He offered further support with his quiet, warm presence once they were in bed, when Ruth whispered, "Please, *Gott*, let him be happy. I bow to Your will, but pray that Your will is also that Malachi be happy. Even if I won't be the one to make him so."

Midmorning the following day, Ruth apprehensively stepped into the Dew Drop Inn, the piece of paper with the names and numbers Mr. Morrow had mentioned clenched tightly in her hand. She'd gone to work early to ease the guilt of leaving briefly when she hoped the traffic at the restaurant was slower. When she'd mumbled her request for an unscheduled break to Malachi, she'd kept her eyes downcast. Ruth couldn't look at him. It hurt too much. He, too, seemed more than usually subdued in his response, although he'd murmured an agreement to her request.

It was the first time she'd seen him after her call to Mr. Morrow.

Much to her surprise, there was already a note addressed to her when she reached the counter in the relatively quiet restaurant. It was from one of Mr. Morrow's contacts, wanting to talk with her. With more dismay than excitement, Ruth discovered when she returned his call that Mr. Morrow had already phoned the numbers and told them of her. The man on the line wanted to talk to Ruth about a job. He was sure she'd be an asset to his operation. He'd arrange for a car to drive her to Madison, about forty miles away. When could she come for an interview?

With closed eyes, Ruth remembered Malachi holding Leah's hand and his stilted interaction with Ruth this morning. She started to tell the man she could come up this afternoon if he could arrange the transportation, and even stay for a while. But when she lifted her eyes, she saw Hannah through the café window, exiting the shop where she worked across the street. Hannah, who'd invited her to tomorrow's cookie exchange.

Ruth's eyes darted around the restaurant and the street outside, noting the Amish people, obvious in their Plain garb, who dotted her line of sight. They were her friends and neighbors. A wave of longing washed over her. She wanted to spend Christmas in Miller's Creek. This one last time. Next year she might be putting up lights and decorations in Madison as the *Englisch* did. Or driving through Wisconsin's winter countryside in a car instead of a buggy, but this year she wanted to celebrate the birth of *Gott*'s son in the Plain way as she had all her life. She clutched the hard plastic of the phone and in a voice not much above a whisper, asked the Madison businessman if after Christmas would be agreeable to him.

After he'd happily concurred, Ruth returned to work on shaky legs. When she stepped back into the workshop, a quick glance located Malachi. He searched her eyes with an enigmatic gaze before she dropped hers and hurried to hang up her cape and get to her current project.

Malachi didn't come near her the rest of the morning. Wanting to avoid her coworkers at lunch, Ruth took her brown bag to the shop where Hannah worked and ate with her friend. That afternoon, she resisted the temptation to look up every time the door opened, just in case it might be him.

Sometime back, Malachi had told Ruth that if he was already in the office, he'd take care of customers that stopped in. Ruth didn't know if she should rejoice or regret that the practice gave her less opportunity to see him. And more for any other women who stopped by the store.

Stop it! She forced her focus to the woodwork before her. Capable hands moved slowly over the wood as she realized in them was the last piece she'd make for what used to be Fisher Furniture. At the pace she was going, she might not finish it before she left the business. And she was going to be gone tomorrow for the cookie exchange.

Ruth bit her lip when she recalled she hadn't yet asked Malachi for time off the next day. She bored the screw hole she was working on more fiercely than necessary as she justified that Amish businesses normally closed on Thursday anyway. In fact the store was closed. The workshop stayed open Thursdays, because business had increased to the point they were frequently pressed for time. Which meant Malachi could be in the workshop all day.

Ruth jutted her chin. She'd worked Thursdays for years. She deserved at least one off. Glancing around the familiar shop, Ruth took in the all the equipment she'd worked on and might never work on again, some she'd had a part in purchasing. Her chin sank in conjunction with her heart. She might as well just take the day. Her absence wouldn't matter in a short time anyway.

When the door opened again, Ruth looked up to meet Malachi's gaze. Something in her expression must have indicated that she wanted to talk, as he leisurely but steadily worked his way in her direction. With every step closer he came, Ruth's mouth grew drier and her palms more sweaty. Wiping them down her apron, she turned to face him.

"Ja?" His eyebrow quirked in his otherwise impassive face.

"I need to be gone tomorrow."

Malachi was quiet for a moment after her blunt statement. Even when she'd just met him and was determined not to like him, Malachi's eyes had always seemed approachable and steady. Now they were cold and distant.

"Seems like you're planning to be gone permanently soon."

Ruth winced. She was hoping he wouldn't know of her plans already. Without phones and electricity, news still flowed through the Amish community with the speed of a breaking dam. She recalled the lingering discussion of Samuel and Rebecca behind her in the restaurant when she'd been on the phone. Apparently the Schrock charmer had ears on him as well as a mouth. Well, delaying the news wasn't going to sweeten it any. Besides, didn't Malachi have an upcoming wedding to participate in?

"*Ja.* Mr. Morrow called one of his business associates. They left a message for me at the Dew Drop. They're sending a car to pick me up so I can go to Madison and talk to them."

His eyes never left hers. "When?"

It was her turn to swallow. She looked away. "I told him not until after Christmas." Ruth saw him nod in her peripheral vision. When she faced him again, he was studying the project she'd been working on.

"You can be gone tomorrow if you're in position to get this done before you leave the business."

Ruth's eyes widened. "But there's not enough time!"

"Whose problem is that? You're the one dictating the schedule." He gestured to the pieces of oak around her. "This project was contracted under Fisher Furniture. You told the customer the availability date. Everyone else is working on other pieces with time constraints. If you don't get it finished, you'll be the one responsible for disappointing the customer. If you don't like the time frame, do something about it."

Ruth glared at him. Approachable and steady? Ha! His eyes weren't cold now; they were almost as heated as hers were.

"All right. I will." Turning her back on what she'd once foolishly thought was an endearing face, Ruth returned to work with renewed vigor. Refusing to do less than her best on her craft, she worked the rest of the afternoon with almost maniacal focus. She didn't look up when the men started removing their coats from the rack and going out the door.

Feeling a gaze on the back of her *kapp*, Ruth finally glanced over, surprised to see Samuel's amused eyes regarding her instead of the blue ones she'd braced herself to meet.

"Still working?"

"No, thanks to you," she groused, returning her attention to the bench while she wondered just what level of violence was allowed on a tattletale in a nonviolent culture. Ruth shot him a glare, figuring that'd be within the limits.

Samuel shook his head. An attractive smile she wanted to wipe off his face creased his cheek. "It'll be okay," he promised as he stepped out the door.

"Lot that you know," she muttered to the now-closed door.

It was some time later when Malachi came through the workshop. He regarded her for a few moments, wisely refraining from commenting.

"I know how to lock up," she tossed over her shoulder. Her eyes, but not her attention, were still on the project in front of her.

There were a few beats of silence. "You have a ride home?"

"I'll get there." Ruth scrunched up her face. She would not cry. Again. Turning to the row of shelves on her opposing side, she blindly selected a wooden dowel she didn't need so he wouldn't see the quiver in her lip. Fortunately it wasn't evident in her voice. "I can take care of myself."

"Never doubted it," were the quiet words she heard prior to the thud of the door closing.

Ruth replaced the dowel and sucked in a deep breath.

Wishing and wanting and hoping and crying weren't going to do her any good. Neither in the short term tonight, nor the long term. Which—she heaved another sigh—seemed very long and bleak at this point. Now that things were in motion for her to leave, she understood what her *daed* had made her promise. He hadn't solicited her promise to leave the Amish community to pursue the possibilities in the *Englisch* world, as she'd always thought. Maybe she'd misinterpreted his wish because it was what she thought she'd wanted. No, he'd made her promise to consciously make a choice—whatever it was—and not just to stay due to expectations or lack of ambition.

Although he'd talked of missed opportunities, Ruth remembered the smile and the loving look in his eyes whenever he spoke of the *mamm* she never knew. He'd had a choice. He'd chosen to stay.

And she was leaving, when every fiber of her being wished that wasn't the case.

Chapter Seventeen

Casting an eye at the skylights that provided most of the light for the shop, Ruth gauged she had about another hour before it would be too dark to work by natural light. A quick search revealed the oil lanterns were still stored where she used to keep them. She grabbed a couple, confirming the oil levels were enough for her to get through the work she needed to finish tonight.

Several hours later, Ruth rolled her shoulders and tipped back her stiff neck. Fueled by hurt and anger—and the internal debate that she shouldn't be feeling those things as she was still Amish, for the next few days anyway—she'd made more progress than she'd hoped. The project would be finished before she left. After Christmas. Ruth mentally pushed out her departure a few more days. The man in Madison would surely understand.

Donning her cape, she stepped out the door and secured it. Ruth hurried toward the Dew Drop Inn, hoping she hadn't left it too late to use their phone to call for a ride. Luckily an *Englisch* business kept later hours than an Amish-owned one. Her relief was as weighty as her tired shoulders when she saw the lights were still on. Even better, the Thompsons were just cashing out at the counter. They gladly agreed to give Ruth a ride.

A short time later, she waved them off from her front step. Ruth had never been so glad to be home. She opened the door to the familiar kitchen, and as she stepped in, she was reminded that she wouldn't be returning to its welcoming walls for long. Her hip sagged against the counter. Yes, it had been lonely here lately, but not so much since...

Ruth dashed back out the door. Snow crunched under her feet as she raced as fast as she dared across the frozen farmyard to the chicken coop. In her frustration and irritation tonight, she'd forgotten all about Rascal. He was probably starving. It was long past his dinnertime.

Ruth slowed her charge when no black-and-white bundle met her at the gate. Quickly unlatching it, she rushed through to enter the coop, hoping to see the pup just waking from a nap. In her haste, she'd forgotten a lamp or a flashlight, but the silence in the dark coop told her it was empty. She called anyway, her pitch rising with each unanswered holler. Making her way to the door, she stumbled into the fenced pen, its emptiness obvious in the moonlit night.

Pressing her fist against her mouth, Ruth bit down on a frozen knuckle to keep from wailing in distress. She slumped against the fence that enclosed the small pen. The woven wire screeched in the cold night air as it gave slightly under her weight.

"Oh, Malachi. I need you. I might be able to take

care of myself, but I don't want to anymore." She couldn't hold back the tears any longer. Her finger rose to wipe under her runny nose. "I'm so tired of taking care of everything. And obviously I'm not doing a good job of it." The tears didn't do any good. Neither did her cry to Malachi. He wasn't there. Even if she had a horse that wasn't recovering from lameness, he was miles away. And might not be alone.

But then, neither was she. Numbly, Ruth looked up to see the endless stars that sprinkled the winter night sky. Blurry at first, they cleared as she blinked the tears away. She felt small. But not alone.

"Gott," she whispered, absorbing the immenseness. "I've been acting for too long like I could manage by myself. And neglecting to ask Your will. Forgive my *hochmut*." Ruth winced at the many times she'd pursued her will instead of asking for *Gott*'s. "I pray for the peace You promise. For I can't do it alone. I know that now, what You've known all along."

Her gaze dropped to the pen, taking in its emptiness. "And, *Gott*, if it is not too much trouble, please look to one little puppy tonight, as well."

Ruth sagged further against the fence, her chin dropping against her chest. While her body felt drained of energy, her mind was curiously relieved. For a few moments, she just breathed. Took in the brisk, clean air, felt the cold at the end of her nose and against her cheeks where the tears had run. She didn't hear anything on the crystal clearness of the night but the beat of her own heart. And Ruth knew it would be all right. Whatever happened. For *Gott* had finally shown her *gelassenheit*. Ruth almost wept anew at the calm spirit that filled her because she'd yielded to His will and not her own.

Opening her eyes, she gazed unseeingly at the yard of the coop. Unseeing, at first. There were puppy tracks throughout the yard where Rascal romped. Paths packed down due to frequent travel. Generally, he didn't get close to the fence, except for the gate. Ruth's gaze sharpened as she took in the ground beneath the end of her cape, where the fence leaned back under her weight. Around her feet, the border of fresh snow had been kicked back. A sprinkling of dirt dug up by paws with sharp little nails topped the dislodged snow. Ruth squatted and found a small hole burrowed under an area of the fence where the bottom wire curled up. Small, but big enough to accommodate an escaping puppy.

The cold metal of the fence squealed again as she pushed off it and whipped out the gate. Dashing into the house, Ruth grabbed a flashlight and a shawl to drape over her cape. Returning to the pen, she followed puppy-size tracks from the fence until they disappeared in the worn ruts in the snow that traced over the farmyard. Heart pounding, Ruth headed down the lane, afraid of what she might find in the ditch.

A light, visible in the darkness that cloaked the rural landscape, was bobbing along the road toward her. It turned into the lane when Ruth was halfway down. In the moonlight reflected on the snow, she could see a black-and-white bundle leap from a black-cloaked figure and race the short distance toward her. Excited yips accompanied each stride.

Hurrying forward to sweep Rascal up into her arms,

Ruth laughed as he licked the traces of tears from her face. "Yes! I'm very glad to see you, as well. Although you gave me quite a fright."

"*Ach*, we'll apologize for that." Ruth identified the black-cloaked forms as the neighbor girls. "He showed up at our place late this afternoon. We didn't know how he got out. We figured he'd find the same way again if we left him, so we waited until you got home to bring him over," Mary, the older of the two sisters, explained. "We thought we'd see a buggy come up the lane, but it wasn't until the car lights flashed as they turned that we knew you'd come home that way." Emma, the younger sister, nodded as she reached out to give the pup's back a long stroke.

Ruth rested her cheek against Rascal's warm head. "It's fine. I'm just glad he's safe. And you are right. He dug a hole under the fence and escaped." She waved the girls farewell and watched as they made their way back down the lane and road to their nearby farmstead.

Much as she wanted to continue hugging him to her, Ruth set the puppy, who was now squirming, down. She turned to head up the lane. "Oh, Rascal. I was so afraid. But you also helped me realize something. Something I needed to determine a long time ago. I knew it, but I didn't live it. You and me, we may think we're independent, maybe even alone, but we're not. *Gott* has always been with us. Even though I might attempt to grab the reins from Him occasionally, I'm going to try to let Him drive."

Ruth inhaled a deep breath of the crisp night air. "Especially over the roads we'll travel for the next while. In the meantime—" Ruth opened the door to the kitchen and the puppy bounded through "—we'll take care of Bess, and after that we have a lot of cookies to make before tomorrow."

Ruth waved Hannah off as her friend drove the pony cart back down the lane. Over Ruth's objections, Hannah had insisted on giving her a ride home after the cookie exchange. Although she attended church every other Sunday, Ruth forgot how wonderful it was to fellowship with her neighbors in the Amish community. Or maybe it was just her new outlook that made her so joyful. Perhaps the fact that her time with them was short had made the outing so precious. Whatever it was, she'd lingered and visited until Hannah proclaimed it was too late for Ruth to walk back and requested that her brother prepare the pony and cart.

A basket of cookies weighed heavy on her arm as she turned away from the lane. The smile that curved her lips faltered as she realized no miniature barking had greeted neither her nor the unfamiliar cart. A rapid glance revealed an empty chicken run. The basket almost dropped to the snow when she saw that the gate was open. Ruth's heart began to pound. Had Rascal gotten loose again? Or had Mary and Emma come and gotten the puppy? She didn't mind the girls playing with the pup, but she wished they'd mentioned it when they left the exchange earlier this afternoon. Ruth's eyes flew to the road in the gathering darkness to see if a light was bobbing its way in her direction.

Frantically, she rushed to the house to get the flashlight and begin a search, only slowing when she saw a glow from the kitchen window. She, like other Amish folks, never locked their homes. It could be anyone in the house. Ruth's heart rate accelerated further. No one but Hannah, who'd just left, had visited her lately. The doorknob in the chilly Wisconsin twilight was frigid in Ruth's sweaty hand. Before she pushed open the kitchen door, she looked back over her shoulder to confirm there wasn't a rig in the shadowed farmyard. There'd been little fresh snow since Bess went lame, so the tracks that crisscrossed the ground leading to the barn could be hers, or someone who'd brought her home. Whoever was in the house could have put their horse and buggy in the barn. But why? Brows furrowed, Ruth hesitantly opened the door.

The glow from the fireplace and an oil lamp on the counter outlined a figure sitting in a chair. Only a quick grab saved the basket from sliding down Ruth's arm and onto the floor. Dazedly, she set it on the counter with a soft thud. Rascal, seated on the lap in the chair, launched himself off and scurried to greet her.

Ruth crouched to the puppy that danced about her feet, gathered him in her arms and rose before meeting a gaze that regarded her warily.

"I am so glad to see you," she murmured to Rascal as she rubbed his ears. "I was so afraid when I thought you might be gone again." The room was quiet after her whisper, the only sounds the occasional pop in the cheerily burning fireplace.

"I was feeling the same way." Malachi's low baritone finally broke the silence. "I didn't know if you'd gone to Madison after all."

Ruth's heart beat faster than the little one whose rapid patter she could feel clutched against her chest.

She tucked the comforting silky head under her chin and met Malachi's gaze. The pup squirmed when trapped between the deep breath she inhaled and her tight grip. "It was a *gut* day today. I didn't want to leave."

"Then why are you?" His voice was equally quiet.

Needing a moment, she placed Rascal on the floor. He shook himself before trotting over to lie down in front of the fireplace. Ruth wished she could shake things off so easily. She lifted her eyes again to his steady blue gaze. "I can't stay in Miller's Creek if you're not free." She forced a swallow. "Are you?"

Malachi didn't answer for a few endless heartbeats. "No, I'm not," he finally responded without breaking eye contact.

It was what she feared and expected. She propped an elbow on the counter to keep from sagging against it. When she thought she could speak, Ruth murmured, "Then what are you doing here?"

"I came to offer you something." In an easy movement, he rose from the chair he was in. Her eyes only for him, Ruth hadn't noticed it. Still gliding smoothly after his abrupt departure was the red oak rocking chair started by her father, a man she'd loved dearly. And now it sat where she envisioned it by the fire, finished by the man she loved more than she could've imagined.

"Oh, Malachi," she breathed. "It's beautiful." On trembling legs, Ruth moved to the chair and ran her fingers across the satiny back. Her eyes drifted shut, imagining for a moment the smooth surface she was stroking was his cheek. She would treasure the piece as she did the ones her *daed* had made. More so, as it had been made by both men.

She opened her eyes when he spoke. "That's *gut* to hear, but that's not all I'm offering." Malachi faced her, the chair between them. A faint smile touched his lips, but his eyes were still apprehensive.

"What I'm offering is my heart, Ruth. It goes with the chair." He smiled, creating a dimple in his lean cheek. "It went before the chair actually. It went when a stubborn woman came along with the furniture business I acquired." He sucked in a breath and blew it out slowly, his eyes never leaving hers. "So you see, I am not free. I belong to you."

Ruth's grip left the back of the chair. She found herself clasping his strong, calloused, wonderful hands. "But what about Leah? She's perfect."

Malachi snorted softly. "Leah helped me learn a lot about what I wanted in a woman. And what I didn't. I didn't want perfect."

Ruth grinned. "You realize what that says about me."

Malachi smiled and squeezed her fingers gently, not letting her go. "I wanted perfect *for me.* A woman with a talent for managing and for working with wood. And for making me happier than I'd ever imagined I'd be. I know you're who *Gott* has chosen for me. He brought me here to Wisconsin in order to find you." The smile faded a bit when he added, "I'm only hoping that I'm enough for you."

He searched her eyes. When she didn't speak, he continued, "I know you have other options. I know you're capable of succeeding in them. I know that staying in the Plain life would limit what you want for yourself. But I allowed myself to hope."

His lips curved slightly. "When wanting to grow a crop worth harvesting or a furniture piece worth making, some preparations have to be made. The groundwork needs to be laid. I figured this was similar. I contacted the bishop regarding permission to set up one of the outbuildings with woodworking equipment, in case someone would consider marrying me. I'd set it up, so when *kinder* arrive, they'd have a safe place to play as well, while their *mamm* makes furniture, if she'd want to."

Ruth stared at him in surprise.

"And I've found I need to learn more about the business part of ownership. I was never much of a reader." He wrinkled his nose. "Even before I left school, my mind was already on physical work. I learn better by hearing and doing. So if I had a wife who wanted to study and learn—" he flicked his eyes toward paperwork still stacked on the kitchen table "—then maybe teach me, interspersed with a few sweet words, it might be a good thing."

Ruth skirted the rocker so nothing was between them. "I could do that. Most of it anyway." Her lips quirked. "Who's going to say the sweet words?"

"How about if I start out with this? Will you marry me, Ruth?" When she drew back and her eyes grew wide, Malachi continued, "I know you can take care of yourself. But for the few occasions that you might want to lean on someone, I want it to be me."

He let go of one of her hands long enough to dab at

a tear that leaked from her eye. "It devastates me when you cry," he murmured.

Ruth sniffed. "Oh, Malachi! The first day you walked into the shop, I reminded myself that *Gott* had a plan for me. Foolish me, I tried to make His path fit mine, thinking I knew what I needed to be happy. But He knew me and, of course, knew better. His plan is so much more than I could've ever imagined. Nothing I could ever find in wood or on paper would bring me the joy of being in your arms."

A smile spread across Malachi's face. He pulled her into his warm embrace. "Well, then. Come here."

Resting her head on his strong shoulder, Ruth whispered, just loud enough for him to hear, "There's an Amish proverb that says to choose your love and love your choice." She nestled deeper into his arms. It felt like home. It felt like everything she'd ever wanted. "I choose you, Malachi."

Epilogue

"*Ach*," Malachi stepped through the door and quickly strode to where Ruth stood on a ladder. "You're supposed to making sure she behaves herself, Samuel."

Turning from where he was building a bench against the wall, Samuel shot Ruth a grin and a wink. "That's your responsibility, *bruder*. You're the one who chose such a stubborn, complicated wife in the first place. It's taught me to make sure I choose a biddable woman when I marry."

"That would be your loss. I couldn't imagine anyone else." Malachi carefully lifted Ruth down. As he set her on the ground, their mutual smiles lingered and his hand gently brushed over her burgeoning stomach before taking the screwdriver from her hand.

Malachi turned his attention to the sloped ceiling. "Come over here and help me with this. Might as well get a little more work out of you before your new horse acquisition business has you forgetting all your woodworking skills."

"You'll miss me. I might even miss you." Samuel

crossed to his *bruder* and climbed the ladder. "But you know horses were always my first love."

Malachi handed him the screwdriver. "I know. But you'll always have a place here if you need it."

Now relegated to the floor, Ruth watched Malachi and Samuel work on the skylight. As promised, Malachi was converting the hog house, its occupants long gone, into a workshop. Glancing around at the renovations, Ruth inhaled deeply, relishing the fresh lumber smell that permeated the airy room. She couldn't imagine being any happier. Everything was set up with safety and efficiency in mind for when she'd work out here.

And she would. But not as much as she'd thought. And that was okay. It was here when she wanted or needed it. For as much as she'd wanted and needed the woodworking, she wanted and needed her Amish husband more. Who'd have ever dreamed she'd have both?

Her lips curved as she listened to the brothers bantering as they worked. Malachi looked over at her and smiled. Ruth's heart swelled as she rested her hand on her slightly rounded stomach. A loving husband, a *bobbeli*, a close extended family, work she loved. The words of Jeremiah ran through her mind. *For I know the thoughts that I think toward you, saith the Lord, thoughts of peace, and not of evil, to give you an expected end.*

Tears prickled in the back of Ruth's eyes, ones born of wonder. Who could have expected this marvelous end for her?

Only *Gott*.

* * * * *

If you loved this story,
check out these other Amish stories:

The Amish Widower's Twins *by Jo Ann Brown*
His Suitable Amish Wife *by Rebecca Kertz*
A Perfect Amish Match *by Vannetta Chapman*
Her New Amish Family *by Carrie Lighte*

Available now from Love Inspired!

Find more great reads at www.LoveInspired.com.

Dear Reader,

What you are holding is the realization of a dream!

As soon as I was old enough to fold an 8.5 x 11 paper into a quarter of its size and draw a horse on the front, I have wanted to write stories. It took a little while, and my artistic skills haven't improved any, but God has helped me realize my writing dream. Everything is better when we trust in Him.

My first interaction with Amish life was when I was at a family reunion in Wisconsin near the location of the fictional Miller's Creek. We were playing volleyball while listening to the clip-clop of horse hooves traveling the nearby highway when two buggies pulled into my uncle's property and two young Amish men hopped out to join our game. And that was my introduction to *rumspringa*. I have been intrigued ever since.

I hope you enjoyed Malachi and Ruth's romance. I grew quite fond of them, especially because Ruth was my grandmother's name. I look forward to exploring the relationships of their siblings and friends in Miller's Creek. I hope you'll join me.

Thank you again for the great honor you've given me of reading my first book. May it be only the beginning of a wonderful adventure together.

Jocelyn McClay

"There won't be another bus going that way until the day after tomorrow."

"Are you sure?" Gemma Lapp stared at the agent behind the counter in stunned disbelief.

"Of course I'm sure. I work for the bus company."

She clasped her hands together tightly, praying the tears that pricked the backs of her eyes wouldn't start flowing. She couldn't afford a motel room for two nights.

She wheeled her suitcase over to the bench. Sitting down with a sigh, she moved her suitcase in front of her so she could prop up her swollen feet. After two solid days on a bus she was ready to lie down. Anywhere.

She bit her lower lip to stop it from quivering. She could place a call to the phone shack her parents shared with their Amish neighbors to let them know she was returning and ask her father to send a car for her, but she would have to leave a message.

Any message she left would be overheard. If she gave the real reason, even Jesse Crump would know before she reached home. She couldn't bear that, although she didn't understand why his opinion mattered so much. His stoic face wouldn't reveal his thoughts, but he was sure to gloat when he learned he'd been right about her reckless ways. He had said she was looking for trouble and that she would find it sooner or later. Well, she had found it all right.

No, she wouldn't call. What she had to say was better said face-to-face. She was cowardly enough to delay as long as possible.

She didn't know how she was going to find the courage to tell her mother and father that she was six months pregnant, and Robert Troyer, the man who'd promised to marry her, was long gone.

Don't miss
Shelter from the Storm *by* USA TODAY
bestselling author Patricia Davids,
available September 2019 wherever
Love Inspired® books and ebooks are sold.

www.LoveInspired.com

*When a guide dog trainer becomes a target
of a dangerous crime ring, a K-9 cop and his loyal
partner will work together to keep her safe.*

Read on for a sneak preview of Trail of Danger
*by Valerie Hansen, the next exciting installment
to the* True Blue K-9 Unit *miniseries,
available September 2019 from Love Inspired Suspense.*

Abigail Jones stared at the blackening eastern sky and
shivered. She was more afraid of the strangers lingering
in the shadows along the Coney Island boardwalk than
she was of the summer storm brewing over the Atlantic.

Early September humidity made the salty oceanic
atmosphere feel sticky while the wind whipped loose
tendrils of Abigail's long red hair. If sixteen-year-old
Kiera Underhill hadn't insisted where and when their
secret meeting must take place, Abigail would have
stopped to speak with some of the other teens she was
passing. Instead, she made a beeline for the spot where
their favorite little hot dog wagon spent its days.

Besides the groups of partying youth, she skirted
dog walkers, couples strolling hand in hand and an old
woman leaning on a cane. Then there was a tall man and

enormous dog ambling toward her. As they passed beneath an overhead vapor light, she recognized his police uniform and breathed a sigh of relief. Most K-9 patrols in her nearby neighborhood used German shepherds, so seeing the long floppy ears and droopy jowls of a bloodhound brought a smile despite her uneasiness.

Pausing, Abigail rested her back against the fence surrounding a currently closed amusement park, faced into the wind and waited for the K-9 cop to go by. His unexpected presence could be what was delaying Kiera.

"Come on, Kiera. I came alone, just like you wanted," Abigail muttered.

Kiera had sounded panicky when she'd phoned.

"Here. Over here" drifted on the wind. Abigail strained to listen.

The summons seemed to be coming from inside the Luna Park perimeter fence. That was not good since the amusement facility was currently closed. Nevertheless, she cupped her hands around her eyes and peered through the chain-link fence. It was several seconds before she realized the gate was ajar. *Uh-oh. Bad sign.* "Kiera? Is that you?"

A disembodied voice answered faintly. "Help me! Hurry."

Don't miss
Trail of Danger *by Valerie Hansen,*
available September 2019 wherever
Love Inspired® Suspense books and ebooks are sold.

www.LoveInspired.com

Discover wholesome and uplifting stories of faith, forgiveness and hope.

Join our social communities to connect with other readers who share your love!

Sign up for the Love Inspired newsletter at **LoveInspired.com** to be the first to find out about upcoming titles, special promotions and exclusive content.

CONNECT WITH US AT:

Facebook.com/groups/HarlequinConnection

 Facebook.com/LoveInspiredBooks

 Twitter.com/LoveInspiredBks

LISOCIAL2019